"You didn't give a reason for leaving."

Nate ran a hand over the taut muscles at the back of his neck. "So why don't you tell me now, Callie? Why'd you take off like that, never to be heard from again?"

"I don't know," she said softly.

For a moment he simply stared at her. After all these years, *this* was her answer.

"I don't know," he mimicked. "Bullshit!"

Callie flinched and he realized he'd never raised his voice to her before. He took in a ragged breath, leaning his forehead against the door frame. Callie was one of the most intelligent women he knew. Intelligent women didn't abandon someone without a reason.

So what was hers?

W9-ALK-855

Dear Reader,

People often act in ways that they can't explain. For instance, I have spent my life hopping from task to task, doing a little here, a little there, until the jobs are done. I thought I was a master multitasker—which I am. I also recently learned that ADD runs in our family and I'm a classic case. I adapted to my particular challenge without knowing what it was. Such is the situation with my heroine in *Always a Temp*.

Callie McCarran has a problem staying in one place long enough to put down roots. Like her father, she's a traveler. She works as a journalist and takes temporary jobs when she needs additional income, moving from city to city, job to job. She avoids permanence in all aspects of her life and accepts this as part of her makeup. What she doesn't know is that there may be other reasons she acts the way she does.

Nathan Marcenek, whom Callie had unceremoniously dumped the day after high school graduation, is a stayer—or so he thinks. He's convinced himself, after suffering a devastating accident, that he's happy living in his small hometown and editing the local paper. Then Callie comes back into his life and suddenly he finds himself questioning his decisions and the reasons he made them.

I hope you enjoy Nate and Callie's journeys in *Always a Temp*. Please stop by my Web site at www.jeanniewatt.com or drop me a line at jeanniewrites@gmail.com. I love hearing from readers.

Jeannie Watt

Always a Temp
Jeannie Watt

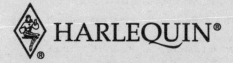

TORONTO • NEW YORK • LONDON
AMSTERDAM • PARIS • SYDNEY • HAMBURG
STOCKHOLM • ATHENS • TOKYO • MILAN • MADRID
PRAGUE • WARSAW • BUDAPEST • AUCKLAND

ISBN-13: 978-0-373-71628-9

ALWAYS A TEMP

www.eHarlequin.com

Printed in U.S.A.

ABOUT THE AUTHOR

Theater usher, gymnastics instructor, grocery store clerk, underground miner, camp cook, geologist, draftsman, executive secretary, groundskeeper, ball-field mower, janitor, teacher, artist, cowboy gear maker, writer. Jeannie Watt has worn many hats, some temporary, some more permanent, during her life. Because of this she knows how to politely ask a parent with a crying baby to step into the lobby without also making the parent cry, how to coax a cranky copy machine into operation, how to jack a loaded mine car back onto the tracks, and how to make breakfast for thirty in a wilderness setting. The skills learned from her many occupations have now become invaluable resources for her favorite job—writing.

Books by Jeannie Watt

HARLEQUIN SUPERROMANCE

Don't miss any of our special offers. Write to us at the following address for information on our newest releases.

Harlequin Reader Service
U.S.: 3010 Walden Ave., P.O. Box 1325, Buffalo, NY 14269
Canadian: P.O. Box 609, Fort Erie, Ont. L2A 5X3

Many thanks to Kimberly Van Meter and Victoria Curran for straightening me out on a number of journalistic points.
Any remaining errors are my own.

I also want to thank Victoria for her patience and insights during revisions.
I knew I needed something more in the story.
Victoria knew what it was.

CHAPTER ONE

THE BOY SCRAMBLED UP and over the fence just as Callie McCarran opened the back door. Sun glinted off his short, silvery-blond hair before he dropped out of sight into the vacant lot next door.

"Hey," Callie called, but it was too late. The kid couldn't be more than seven or eight, but he was a quick little guy. It was the second time she'd seen him in the yard in the two days she'd been back in town, which seemed odd, since there was nothing of interest back here.... But then she noticed the baseball-size hole in the porch screen, which was quite possibly related to the baseball lying under the wicker chair.

Callie bent down to get it.

"I found your ball," she called. Nothing. Shaking her head, she went out into the overgrown grass and set it on the empty birdbath.

"It's on the birdbath," she yelled, in case the kid was crouching on the other side of the fence. "I'm going in the house now." She walked a few steps, then added, "And I'm not mad about the hole." The entire porch needed to be rescreened before she could sell the house, so no big deal.

Callie went back into the classic 1980s kitchen, complete with country-blue ruffled curtains at the windows and cow-decorated canisters on the cream-colored countertops. She poured a glass of tap water and drank it all without setting the glass down. She'd cried a lot during the past few days and no matter how much water she drank, she felt dehydrated. But she had held up during the memorial service, thank goodness, because if she had broken down, the good townspeople would have added "hypocrite" to her list of epithets. They were already treating her like a leper.

Okay, leper was probably too strong of a word. People had been pleasant enough, offering the obligatory condolences, but she'd been aware of the undercurrents, the why-the-hell-weren't-you-there-for-your-foster-mother-in-her-time-of-need undercurrents. And no one spent much time talking to her. A few murmured words, then off to join other more legitimate mourners standing in small groups near the buffet. Following the service, Callie had spent most of the time alone beside the podium, waiting for the moment when she could leave. Grace's accountant had stood with her for a while, but Callie had a feeling that was only because she was paying him, or rather the estate was paying him, to take care of the final bills. Even he eventually drifted away.

Damn it, I would have been there for Grace, if I'd known how sick she was.

She hadn't known…and she hadn't exactly tried to find out, either. Instead she had stayed with her once-in-a-lifetime trip through Kazakhstan. Attached to a geologic field tour, she'd been chronicling the economic growth and environmental pitfalls since foreign companies had been allowed to mine there.

She was still quite angry with Grace for not telling her she was terminal. That while treating her for a chronic stomach disorder, the doctor had discovered an inoperable malignant growth. But really, Callie hadn't wanted to know the truth.

She'd been afraid to know.

The worst part was that she'd ignored the biggest red flag of all: Grace had asked her to come back to Wesley when she returned to the States. She hadn't been home in twelve years, and in hindsight, Callie could see that Grace wouldn't have made such a request without one hell of a good reason—such as being in the process of dying.

Callie refilled the glass and walked to the back door, peering through the window. The ball was still perched on the birdbath. She wondered if the kid would come back or if this was the last she'd see of him. If he did come and get the ball, she hoped he'd play with it somewhere else.

Not that she'd be here.

But then again, maybe she would. For the first time in a long time, Callie felt no desire to move on. No need to find the next city to explore, the next story to write…maybe because she hadn't written anything except her contracted Kazakhstan article since receiving news of Grace's death.

Callie pressed the cool glass to her cheek. This was the second time she'd suffered such a loss, and it wasn't any easier than the first. Just different.

Her father had disappeared when she was six, leaving her with Grace, his distant cousin and only relative. A business trip. Except he'd never returned. Now she'd lost the only other parent she'd even known.

She set the glass in the sink and went to her old bedroom, now a guest room, and pulled her dark blue knit dress over her head and tossed it on the bed. None of her clothes wrinkled. She traveled too much to buy anything that couldn't be crumpled into a ball and shoved into a suitcase. She traveled with only a carry-on bag whenever possible, because she hated dealing with extra baggage. No extra belongings, no extra people. Just the bare minimum.

But Grace hadn't been extra baggage.

Callie sank down onto the bed and stared at the wall opposite. She should have made more of an effort. *Should have, should have, should have…*

The room had been pale green when she'd lived here. She'd wanted lavender, a color Grace could not abide.

Callie had begged, but the room had remained green, because Grace said there was no way she was having that much lavender in her house.

Now the walls were apricot.

Which meant…?

Nothing. It meant that it had been time to paint and Grace had chosen a different color.

Restless, Callie got up and paced back into the living room in her underwear. It was hot and no one was likely to stop by to visit the ungrateful foster child.

A magazine lay folded back on itself on the maple end table next to Grace's blue velvet recliner. Her slippers were on the floor next to the chair. Grace was everywhere and nowhere.

And the house was so freaking quiet.

Callie had to get out. Regain her equilibrium so she could deal with stuff that two weeks ago she had no idea she'd be dealing with.

A few minutes later, dressed in cropped khaki pants, flip-flops and a light pink T-shirt, she all but bolted down the walk. There weren't many places to go in Wesley, Nevada, but she'd find somewhere.

"Callie!" Alice Krenshaw was standing on her porch next door, still wearing the black muumuulike dress she'd worn to the memorial, a copper watering can in her plump hand. "Are you all right?" she asked, probably out of a sense of duty, because she hadn't been friendly at the funeral.

"Fine," Callie called back, not slowing her pace. Maybe later she'd talk to Alice, but right now she didn't want to talk to anyone. She saw her shake her head as Callie got into her borrowed Neon, read the disapproval in the gesture.

She started the engine and pulled out onto the street, having no idea where she was going. For the first time…ever…she wasn't entirely sure that being accountable to no one but herself was a good thing.

Right now Callie wouldn't mind leaning on someone, and there was only one person in town who might agree to prop her up, but she had fences to mend there first. A minor repair, she hoped. After all, twelve years had passed, and surely by now Nate would have come to the conclusion that what she'd done had been for the best.

"DID YOU HEAR ME, Mr. Marcenek?"

Nathan Marcenek took off his glasses and rubbed a hand over his eyes, his vision blurry from staring at a computer screen for too long. When he focused on Joy Wong, the receptionist for the *Wesley Star* newspaper, she blinked at him expectantly.

"Callie's here?" He hadn't seen this one coming. In fact, he'd been surprised to hear she'd come back for the service, since she hadn't set foot in Wesley since abruptly leaving town, and him, the day after high school graduation. Even Grace's illness hadn't brought her home.

"Send her in," Nathan said, wishing he'd had the foresight to hide a flask of whisky in his desk drawer for occasions such as these. He had a feeling he might want a stiff belt after this unexpected meeting was over.

Joy nodded and disappeared into the hall. He heard her say, "First door on the left," and then a moment later the woman he could have quite happily gone the rest of his life without seeing again walked into his office. And if anything, she was more striking than he remembered.

Her dark blond hair was shorter than it'd been in high school, curving along her shoulders instead of falling down her back, and the freckles over her nose had faded. But her eyes were the same. Closer to aqua than blue; her gaze direct and candid. Or so it seemed. Nathan had learned the hard way that Callie was a master at hiding things.

"Hi, Nate," she said, her voice husky.

"Callie." He stood, his leg protesting the movement less than usual. Adrenaline mixed with testosterone was amazing stuff. "It's been a while," he said, uttering the understatement of the year. He sat back down without offering his hand or cheek, or whatever one offered to an ex-friend/girlfriend who'd proved to be less than trustworthy, and gestured to the chairs on the other side of the desk.

Callie appeared unfazed by his lack of warmth. She would have been a fool if she had expected him to welcome her with open arms and Callie was anything but a fool.

She took a seat on the only chair that didn't have papers or books stacked on it, and set her small leather backpack on the tiled floor next to her feet. When she focused on him again, her expression was more businesslike, as if she'd changed tactics, which instantly put him on edge. Tactics meant a mission, and Nathan wasn't going to be involved with any Callie missions.

"I was surprised to hear you were editing the *Star*," she said as she folded her hands in her lap, obviously more comfortable with this reunion than he was. "The last I'd heard you were working as a reporter in Seattle."

So she knew something about his career. Nathan waited, wondering if she was also aware that he'd been injured on that particular job. Rather spectacularly injured, in fact. The story had gone national, but the incident had been followed almost immediately by a huge government scandal that had stolen the headlines for weeks.

Callie waited for his reply to her small-talk opening, and after a few seconds he began to relax. She didn't know. There would be no token murmurs of sympathy. No suspicions that he'd tried to live in the fast lane and had gotten the snot knocked out of him. Callie was the last person he wanted to know about that, since honestly, the way she'd dumped him without ever looking back had been part of the reason he'd tried to be less boring.

"I took this job fourteen months ago."

"Where were you before that?"

"Here and there. How about you?" he asked, trying to figure out what was going on. Surely she wasn't here cashing in on old-friend status? If so, she was bordering on delusional. Friends were people you could trust. Friends didn't do what she'd done. "Where've you been working?"

The better question would have been where *hadn't* she been working? Callie never stayed in one place long. He hadn't consciously followed her career—pretty much the opposite, in fact—but Grace had been proud of the foster daughter who never came to visit, and made sure everyone knew where Callie was working.

"Same places as you," she replied. "Here and there. Funny we didn't meet." She didn't exactly smile, but the dimple appeared near the corner of her mouth. Even now it charmed the hell out of him, which in turn ticked him off.

"Yeah." The polite game was over. He didn't smile back, but instead held her gaze, waiting for her to explain the reason for her visit as he absently rubbed the muscles of his right thigh.

Callie sat in stubborn silence on the other side of his desk, studying him. He wondered how he was stacking up to the guy she'd dumped after graduation. Finally, he gave in and said, "I'm sorry about Grace."

"Thank you. It was a shock."

Nathan didn't try to hold back the snort. The culmination of a terminal cancer diagnosis had been a shock? That pissed him off. "She'd been sick for a long time," he pointed out none too gently. "Where were you?"

The color left her cheeks, but her eyes flashed. "I didn't know about the cancer, all right?"

He guessed he shouldn't have been surprised, although he found it hard to believe that none of Grace's friends had tried to contact her. "Did you try to find out?"

"She told me she was doing fine, that they'd just changed her treatments. I thought I had time to finish the project I was working on." Callie cleared her throat, the first indication that perhaps she wasn't as cool and collected as she wanted him to believe. "If I'd had any idea how serious it was, I would have been here."

Nathan wondered. He took off his reading glasses, holding them by the bow. "So," he said briskly, making the change of topic sound like a brushoff, "once the estate is settled, where are you heading off to?"

"Nowhere."

His jaw tightened. He didn't want her in town, didn't want to be around her. Didn't like being reminded of those days when he'd gone through hell wondering why she'd left. Why she wouldn't take his calls. Not the best of times for a kid who was struggling with self-image issues, issues his dad wasn't exactly helping him with.

"You're keeping the house?" His voice was amazingly cool considering what his blood pressure was doing.

She drew back at the suggestion. "Of course not. I just want some…" Her voice trailed off as she made a small gesture. A fire opal set in an asymmetrical gold band on her left ring finger caught the light. An engagement ring? Somehow he doubted it. "I want some time to go through Grace's things. Tidy up the place to sell. I don't have any pressing commitments."

"I see." And he now had an idea of what was coming next. If she wasn't here as an alleged friend, then…

"I need a temporary job, Nate. I don't want to live solely on savings."

Bingo.

She leaned forward in her chair, her expression intent. "I thought I could freelance for you." When Nathan didn't answer immediately, she added, "I might even improve circulation."

Heaven knew she'd improved his circulation more than once. Nathan shoved the thought aside. "Yeah, you would do an excellent job. There's just one problem."

"That I'll be leaving?"

He set his glasses on top of a stack of papers, rubbed his eyes again. "That's not the problem."

"Then what, Nate?"

He hesitated for a moment before he said, "I don't want to work with you, Callie, and I don't want to publish your articles."

Her eyebrows, a few shades darker than her hair, rose higher. "You're kidding."

He shook his head, watching Callie's expression change as she realized he meant what he said. He was passing up work from a writer of her caliber.

"Because of what happened between us," she said.

He nodded. "But that was twelve years ago."

"That doesn't make what you did any less crummy."

Callie showed no emotion as she said, "I'm not here asking for friendship, Nate." But he had a strong feeling that had been exactly what she'd been there for. Callie didn't have any friends left in town. He was all that remained of their small high school group. "I just want to submit some freelance work."

"Isn't going to happen."

"I can't believe you're letting personal matters interfere with professional."

"Believe it, Cal."

"Would you at least give me a chance to—"

"What would it matter?" he asked sharply, cutting her off. "If you had something to explain, maybe you could have answered one of my calls twelve years ago. You know, back when I cared?"

Callie rose to her feet and slung her leather bag over her shoulder so hard it made a noise when it hit her back.

Nathan also stood, and again his leg cooperated.

"Well, I guess I'll see you around." Her voice was cold.

And he probably would see her around for a few days, because she'd make certain he did, but he'd bet his next paycheck she'd be gone within a matter of weeks. Or days. She'd find a new assignment, let the real estate agent sell the house, the accountant handle the estate.

"Goodbye, Callie."

She left without another word, the distinctive sound of her flip-flops echoing on the tile in a weird staccato rhythm as she returned to the main office. Nathan sat back down, stretching out his bad leg, feeling the familiar deep ache as his scarred muscles protested. His nerves were humming.

He'd done a decent job of pushing Callie out of his mind over the years, filing their relationship away under Rugged Learning Experiences. He rarely read her articles and he'd had no intention of ever seeing her again.

Now here she was, back in Wesley, ready to let bygones be bygones. He reached for his glasses.

As he'd said, it wasn't going to happen.

CHAPTER TWO

THANKFULLY, JOY WONG wasn't at her desk when Callie left Nathan's office, because, thick-skinned as she was, Callie didn't think she could handle any more rejection today—not even a dismissive smile. Joy had been one of Grace's friends, although Callie had never known her well, and it had been obvious from her politely distant demeanor at the memorial service that Joy was in the Callie-is-a-rotten-person camp.

Callie quickly skirted the receptionist's desk, crossed the foyer and escaped out of the building into the heat. The big glass door closed behind her with a muffled click.

Safe.

She couldn't believe how off base she'd been about Nate.

The plan had been simple when she'd entered the *Wesley Star* office. She would apologize to Nate for running scared, explain that she'd been overwhelmed by things she still didn't fully understand. And then Nate, realizing that she'd been young and confused, and obviously had a reason for not contacting him, would forgive her. After all, twelve years had passed. Time heals all wounds and all of that. But two seconds into the reunion Callie knew she'd better come up with a different plan. The young Nate she'd jilted was nothing like the older Nate sitting behind the editor's desk. Oh, they looked almost the same—dark-haired, blue-eyed, with glasses—but they weren't the same guy. So she'd saved face and pretended she was interested in freelancing, which she was, never dreaming that Nate would reject her there, too.

She felt like crap.

Heat waves danced on the asphalt as Callie crossed the lot to her car. She didn't even look at the man loading equipment into a minivan two spaces away from where she was parked. He seemed vaguely familiar, but she wasn't going to submit herself to more rampant disapproval.

Callie opened the car door with a little too much force, making the old hinges squeak, and climbed into the two-hundred-degree interior, cranking the windows down as soon as she shut the door. Since she rarely needed a car, unless she happened to be making a trip across the Nevada desert to a place with no airport, she didn't own one. The Neon belonged to a friend of a friend in Berkeley, who'd had no qualms about lending it to Callie indefinitely in exchange for two hundred dollars—which was approximately twice the value of the cranky little car, as near as she could tell.

Callie pulled the neck of her shirt away from her damp skin before she reached for the ignition. The no-frills Neon lacked AC, and she was getting a quick refresher course in just how hot Nevada could be in August. Even the high desert, where Wesley was located, had long stretches of days in the hundred-degree-plus range, and wasn't she lucky that they were having one now?

As she pulled away from the building, she glanced at Nate's window. He was sitting there staring at his computer. It killed her how much he looked the same, yet how different he was. Of course, there were small changes that came with maturity. His face had become leaner, making his cheekbones more prominent, his chin more angular. And his body was harder, more muscular. Ironically, he'd been dressed almost exactly the same the last time she'd seen him, on graduation night, right down to the sleeves of his oxford shirt rolled up over his forearms and his shirt tucked into jeans rather than pants. He'd once told her that the only thing that stood between him and complete nerddom was that he refused to give up his Levi's. She'd never thought of him as a nerd, but rather as the quiet brother sandwiched in between two hell-raisers. Safe, dependable, understanding Nate… Scratch understanding.

Yeah, Nate had changed.

A few minutes later she parked her car in front of Grace's house, which, once the estate was settled, would be hers.

Callie McCarran. Home owner.

What a joke. Houses were for people who liked to put down roots, form relationships. Other people signed mortgages and long-term leases. Callie paid rent on a mouse-proof storage unit to store the few things she treasured and could not bring with her on her travels.

A house would be wasted on her.

CHIP ELROY POKED HIS shaved head into Nathan's office. "Hey, was that Callie McCarran I saw leaving the building a while ago?" He had two cameras hanging around his neck and a large black lens bag in one hand.

"In the flesh," Nate muttered, looking back down.

"Wow. I haven't seen her since high school." Chip gave a slight cough. "She, uh, filled out nicely, wouldn't you say?"

"Yes," Nathan said in a conversation-stopping tone. "Do you have something you need to discuss?"

"Nope," Chip answered, emphasizing the *p* and taking the hint. "I'm heading out to take photos of the new bridge." He pushed off from the door frame, his baggy pants dropping an inch as he did. He hiked them back up with his free hand.

"Are you done with the BLM story?"

"I will be by tomorrow morning."

"See to it." Nathan shifted back to the piece he was editing. It would be so great if Chip had a clue when to use an apostrophe. At least he took decent photos.

Two hours and one headache after Callie had left, Joy came into Nathan's office carrying a cup of green tea. She insisted he drink one cup a day to help combat stress. Nathan actually thrived under pressure and hated green tea, which tasted like boiled lettuce, but he was wise enough not to mess with Joy. The office would implode without her.

"Thanks," he said absently as she set the cup on the one clear spot on his desk—the spot he kept clear for this purpose—close to the potted plant. He was beginning to think that there might be something to the purported medicinal properties of green tea, since the dieffenbachia had put on an amazing growth spurt.

"You should have hired her to freelance," Joy said. There was no doubt which "her" she meant, since with the exception of Millie, the advertising salesperson, there had been no other woman in the office that day.

Nathan looked up. "You were listening?"

"Not on purpose. You didn't close the door and I was in the supply closet taking inventory. You should have given her some work."

"But I didn't."

"It would have reduced the load here."

"She's going to be gone in a few weeks, Joy."

"How do you know?" Joy challenged.

Nathan moved his mouse, bringing his screen back up. "Trust me. I know."

"We'll see," she replied on her way out the door,

which she closed behind her, leaving Nathan free to dispose of his tea and to wonder why she was defending Callie. Since Joy and Grace had been friends, he hadn't expected that. And he hadn't made a mistake.

Vince Michaels, the owner of the *Wesley Star* and several other rural papers scattered throughout Nevada and western Utah, would not agree. He'd be totally pissed if he discovered that Nathan had refused to hire Callie, since she'd won a few awards and people knew her name.

Was that why he felt like hell?

"WHAT ARE YOUR SKILLS?" Mrs. Copeland, the woman who managed the only temp agency in Wesley, propped her fingertips together as she asked the question. Tech Temps catered almost solely to the gold mining industry, the number one employer in northern Nevada, but Callie was more than willing to take on a mine job, which ranged from secretarial to truck driving. Two days had passed since her unsettling conversation with Nate, and she still had no idea what she was going to do in the future. But if she was going to stay in Wesley for an undetermined amount of time, then she needed to work, because at the moment, writing wasn't cutting it.

If she had to, she could write the service articles her magazine contacts were asking her to take on, but Callie's strength was her voice. She wrote about people and places and her unique style had earned her both a name and a steady income.

Now, not only was her writing off, her voice was MIA and she was getting concerned. She hoped that if she got out into the workforce, met new people, had new experiences, something would spark, as it always had before, and the words would flow once again.

Grief was a bitch.

"I can do just about anything." And she had, having supported herself with temporary jobs, between travel writing and other freelance gigs, since she'd left college. Indeed, the list of Callie's skills, noted on the résumé sitting in front of Mrs. Copeland, was long and detailed. Maybe that was why the woman wasn't looking at it.

Mrs. Copeland puckered her mouth thoughtfully and turned to her computer. She clicked her mouse and made a face. "Diesel mechanic?"

Callie couldn't help smiling. "No, that's one area where I'm lacking, but I did work in a tire store once."

"Accounting?"

"At first, but one of the regular guys got sick for a week, so I mounted tires and fixed flats."

Mrs. Copeland clicked through several more screens, her expression not exactly reassuring.

"Anything?" Callie had already checked the local paper, which was her only source of employment information. A remote town like Wesley had no short-term job listings on the Internet boards.

"Doesn't look good. Most temp jobs are seasonal and you're here at the end of the summer rather than the beginning."

"I was hoping someone had become conveniently pregnant and needed time off."

"It happens," Mrs. Copeland mused. But it didn't look as if it was happening now. Callie felt a sinking sensation when the lady took her hand off the mouse and turned to her, propping her elbows on her desk and clasping her fingers under her chin. "I see you have a college degree."

"In journalism." But she had a sneaking suspicion there wasn't a big call for journalists in the mining industry.

"I suggest you go to the school district office. They're crying for subs."

"Subs?"

Callie's horror must have shown. Subbing involved kids, and she hadn't spent much time around kids. Like, none. The woman smiled. "It's not a bad job. They pay close to a hundred dollars a day. You work from eight to three forty-five."

"Then why are they crying for subs?" A justifiable question, considering the high pay and the short hours.

"They require two years of college to get the license and not many people here meet that requirement. If they do, they usually have full-time jobs."

"A hundred dollars a day."

"Almost a hundred," Mrs. Copeland corrected her, her chin still resting on her clasped hands.

"I was hoping for something steadier." Even a serial temp worker needed a little security in the short term.

"Trust me, it's steady. My brother teaches and I know." Mrs. Copeland picked up Callie's résumé and slid it into a manila folder. "If you're not interested in subbing," she said, after placing the folder on a high stack on the rolling file cabinet next to her, "you can check back every few days, or check online. Maybe something will open up."

"Okay. Thanks." Callie left the office and walked to her hot car. Subbing…did she want to get back in the workforce that badly?

She gave herself a shake. Okay. The idea of trying to control a class of kids was intimidating, especially since she had zero notion how to do that, but…if it didn't work out, she didn't have to go back. Heck, if it didn't work out, she probably wouldn't be allowed back. She would go with Plan B then—taking the magazine contracts. She didn't want to do that just yet because a small part of her was afraid that was all she'd ever do from that point on. She might never write anything worthwhile again.

Callie got into the Neon and drove the half mile to the school district office, where they practically hugged her for showing up with a bona fide college diploma and the desire—although Callie wasn't quite certain that was the correct word—to substitute teach. These people were desperate.

After filling out forms and getting instructions on what to do with transcripts, she went to the sheriff's office to be fingerprinted—a requirement for the sub license application. She'd looked around cautiously when she arrived, since once upon a time Nate's father, John Marcenek, a man who'd never particularly cared for Callie, had been sheriff. But surely he'd retired by now. He had to be over sixty.

"Who's sheriff?" Callie asked the brisk woman wearing too much perfume who took the prints.

"Marvin Lodi."

Callie wasn't familiar with the name. "John Marcenek retired then?" She was actually kind of hoping he'd been voted out of office.

"Yes. He's chief of the volunteer fire department now."

That sounded like the perfect retirement gig for Nathan's dad. Something where he could be in command and throw his weight around.

Callie left the sheriff's office and went back to Grace's house, where she ordered her college transcript online, requesting that it be sent directly to the State Department. The extreme shortage of subs in the district meant her application would be expedited, according to the district office secretary. As soon as the paperwork was approved, all she had to do was wait for a call.

And in the meantime, she could try to force out some words.

Callie went into the kitchen with its sparkling lino-leum floor, waxed in a bout of insomnia the night before, and glanced out the back window at the grass she needed to mow as soon as it cooled off. Then she smiled.

The baseball, which had disappeared from the birdbath a few hours after she'd put it there two days ago, was back, next to her bottom step. She went outside and picked it up, wondering if the owner was anywhere nearby.

The fence separating her property from the alley and the vacant lot next door was solid wood, but on the other side chain-link divided the backyards, so Callie was able to see Alice Krenshaw pruning her bushes near the corner of her house.

"Hey, Alice," she called, her first voluntary contact since the memorial. She figured if they were going to be neighbors, however temporary, then they needed to develop a working relationship.

Alice looked up from under the brim of her garden-ing bonnet, her pruning shears still open, prepared for the next snip. "Do you know a little white-haired kid in the neighborhood?"

"He lives in the rental on the other side of the vacant lot. The Hobarts." Alice pointed to the two-story house, which was a bit ramshackle, with worn paint and missing screens.

"Thanks. I need to return something." Callie held

up the baseball and Alice nodded before returning to her pruning.

Callie went through the back gate into the alley, half expecting to find a kid crouched in the shadow of the fence, waiting for the opportunity to retrieve his ball. She walked along the buckled asphalt to the house Alice had pointed out. The backyard wasn't fenced and the weeds of the lot that separated the house from Grace's were encroaching into the dried grass. A few toys were scattered about—a yellow dump truck and bulldozer, a half-deflated plastic swimming pool. Dead bugs and leaves floated on the remaining water.

No kids.

Callie looked up at the second floor windows and clearly saw two children looking down at her—the white-haired boy and a darker blonde girl. Callie held up the ball and they both instantly disappeared from view. But they didn't come out the back door as she expected. She waited for several minutes, and when it became obvious that she could be cooling her heels for nothing, she walked down the alley and around to the front of the house, where she rang the doorbell. The bell made no sound, so she knocked. And knocked again.

Nothing happened.

Okay... Then it hit her. The kids must be home alone and had been told not to answer the door. It made perfect sense. Callie set the baseball on the weathered porch boards and headed back to her own house.

Maybe she could do a piece on latchkey kids….

NATHAN MOUNTED THE road bike and expertly locked his shoe cleats into the clipless pedals, then started down the road leading out of town. It had not been a good day, with deadlines stacking up like cordwood and a phone call from the big boss, Vince Michaels, insisting that Nathan put Vince's high-school-aged son, Mitch, to work again. Mitch had worked as an intern the previous semester and had been about as useless as a screen door on a submarine. Then to complicate matters, Nathan found out Mitch had been harassing Katie, the part-time billing clerk, with sexual innuendos. Nathan had put a quick stop to that and had called Vince, who hadn't taken the matter seriously until Nathan mentioned the potential for a harassment suit. Then he'd taken notice. Mitch had sulked and stayed away from Katie, but he'd continued to be as useless as ever.

Nathan didn't need Mitch hanging around again, doing nothing and upsetting the people who were actually working, but he had him. Another Vince-related headache. Nathan had a lot of autonomy working at the *Star,* but there were areas where the boss needed to back off and keep his fingers out of the pie.

Nathan geared down as he approached the first big hill, and the tension on the pedals eased as revolutions per minute increased, allowing him to maintain speed as he climbed. The first time he'd ridden after getting out of the hospital, he'd gone all of a mile. His good leg had had to do the work; his injured leg had been along for the ride, the foot locked onto the pedal by the cleat mechanism in his shoe, the leg doing little more than bobbing up and down as the pedals turned. But as time passed, the remaining muscles in that leg started doing their job, and now he rode fifteen to twenty miles a night, sometimes thirty, depending on how late he left the office and how stressed he was. Despite the deadlines, he'd managed to get out relatively early tonight, before seven o'clock, anyway, because Chip had turned in two decent articles, proofread and well written for once.

It was twilight by the time Nathan had completed the loop around the edge of town, dipping down near the river, then back through the older section of town, where he lived. When he rounded the last corner before his house he saw his younger brother, Seth, backing out of the driveway. Seth caught sight of him and pulled the truck forward again.

"Good ride?" he asked, getting out. He had on his wilderness clothes—a light green microfiber shirt, khaki pants, hiking boots. His hat was jammed in his back pocket instead of on his close-cropped, dark blond hair. Out to commune with nature, no doubt. Or to rescue someone. He was driving the official beaten-to-death truck with the SAR—Search and Rescue—insignia on the door.

"Every ride's a good ride," Nathan answered, pulling off his helmet and shaking his sweaty hair. For a while he'd been afraid that he'd never ride again. "What's up?"

"I'm on my way out of town and needed to borrow your GPS." He held it up. "Mine's on the fritz."

"Help yourself to my stuff anytime," Nathan said as he pushed the bike into the garage with one hand on the seat. "You know how much I like it."

"Oh, I will," Seth said with a laugh. "Has Garrett talked to you at all?"

"About?" Nathan hung the bike on a set of supports attached to the wall, hooked his helmet over the bar extender, then peeled off his gloves.

"He's all ticked off about some fight he had with Dad. Don't tell him I told you." Seth started for his truck.

"Hey, he's the one who wanted to live next door to Dad." Nathan was surprised that his dad had fought with Garrett, though. Usually he saved his arguments for Nathan, the kid he didn't understand.

"No. He's the one who wanted to live rent free," Seth corrected, and he had a point, since their father owned the house next door and didn't charge Garrett rent in return for minor property upkeep. "Want anything from the city? I'm stopping in Elko on my way to Jarbidge."

Nathan shook his head. "I'm good. What's going on in Jarbidge?" The isolated mountain community boasted a population of less than a hundred.

"Probably a party, but we're going up for specialized search and rescue training starting early tomorrow morning." Seth got into the truck and was about to close the door when he said conversationally, "You aware that Callie's still in town?"

"I am." His brothers were the only people who knew the truth about what Callie had done to him. As far as everyone else knew, they'd parted by mutual agreement.

"Just wondering," Seth said casually.

"No big deal." Because it wasn't—except that whenever he thought about her coming into his office, cool as could be, his blood pressure spiked. He was really looking forward to the day she put Wesley behind her. Then the coronary he was working on would result from deadlines alone.

As his brother swung out onto the sealed blacktop, Nathan lifted a hand, then went into the house through the side door, hitting the switch to close the garage as he went in. He'd barely peeled out of his sweaty shirt when the town fire siren blew. He grimaced and put the damp shirt back on again. He hated going to fires, but Chip was leaving town for two days, so he was the only one there to cover the story.

He really had to hire another reporter.

But it wouldn't be Callie. He didn't care if she stayed for a decade.

CHAPTER THREE

CALLIE WOKE to the smell of smoke. She pushed her hair back from her forehead as she sat up, disoriented until she realized that, despite the noise of the antique cooling system churning in the window beside her, she'd conked out on the sofa. That would teach her to wax floors at midnight.

She got to her feet, rubbing the crick in her neck as she went out on the front porch. The neighborhood was quiet, but the smell of smoke was strong. She walked out to the middle of the street, where she could see over the tops of the houses, and sure enough, a column of dark smoke rose into the rapidly darkening sky on the north edge of town, where housing developments encroached on the desert and Bureau of Land Management property. It was the season for wildfires, but black smoke meant a structure was burning.

Maybe she'd find something to write about.

Callie went back in the house, ran a comb through her sleep-flattened hair, then grabbed her car keys. By the time she'd followed the smoke to the outskirts of town, about a mile away from Grace's house, several vehicles bearing volunteer firefighter license plates had sailed by her.

A crowd of onlookers gathered on the last street of the development, which had new tract houses on one side and vacant lots on the other. Maybe seventy yards away, on the undeveloped side of the street, firemen were dousing flames that had engulfed a derelict trailer parked in a weed-choked lot.

Ever conscious of not getting in the way of people who had a job to do, because that tended to get one banished from the scene, she parked her car several yards from the closest vehicle, hugging her wheels to the ditch to keep the roadway clear. She left the car and casually walked up to the knot of bystanders, wanting to blend in as she took in the scene.

"Any idea how it started?" she asked the teenager next to her, a sandy-haired kid with baggy pants. The sky was clear, so if the fire had been caused by lightning, it was a freak strike.

The teen shrugged without looking at her, but the middle-aged man standing slightly in front of her turned, frowning as if he was trying to place her. Probably not too many strangers showed up at neighborhood fires, so Callie couldn't blame the guy for thinking she might be a firebug there to enjoy the results of her handiwork.

"I'm Callie McCarran," she said, saving him the

trouble of trying to memorize her face or get her license plate number.

"Doug Jones." He turned back toward the action, but Callie caught him watching her out of the corner of his eye.

Callie gave the teenager another shot. "Have you had many fires this summer?" Fire seasons varied. Some years would be fire-free and during others it would seem as if the entire state was ablaze.

"We've had a few," the boy said without looking at her. His focus was on the firemen—or rather, on one particular fireman who looked as if he might be a she. The only she, as far as Callie could tell.

"Do you know the name of the female firefighter?"

The kid shrugged again and ignored her.

Oh, yeah. She was going to do well substitute teaching. Couldn't get kids to answer the door. Couldn't get kids to answer a question. And speaking of kids… Callie saw a distinctive white head at the edge of the crowd. Her across-the-lot neighbor. This little guy got around. Callie craned her neck to see who was with him, but the crowd shifted and she lost sight of him.

The breeze was light and it didn't take long for the firefighters to get the blaze under control and stop it from spreading to the desert, where it could have taken off in the dry grass, sage and rabbit brush, causing major damage. The crowd started to disperse as the flames died, some people going to cars, others to nearby houses, and Callie once again caught sight of the boy as he tried to resist his sister's efforts to pull him down the street. No adult was in sight and it was nearly nine o'clock. What would two kids that age be doing so far from home?

Unless they had sneaked out to see the action without their parents knowing. Kids did do things like that, or so she'd heard. She'd been too afraid of the wrath of Grace to have tried.

The girl finally got her brother to cooperate, even though she wasn't much bigger than he was, and he began trudging down the street beside her. Every now and then he looked over his shoulder at the firefighters.

Callie wasn't about to offer them a ride, being a stranger and all, and no one else seemed concerned by their presence, so she decided that Wesley was indeed a very small town and the rules were different than in a more urban area. She watched until they pulled their tired-looking bicycles out of the ditch near a streetlight and started riding off along the sidewalk. Okay. They had transportation home. But it still disturbed her to see kids out that late without an adult.

Doug Jones gave Callie one last suspicious look, then headed to a nearby house. *Bye, Doug.* Callie stayed where she was, hoping to get a chance to talk to the female firefighter, who was still dealing with embers near what was left of the trailer.

As she waited, a big Dodge truck and a panel wagon pulled out of the throng of vehicles belonging to the volunteers, giving Callie a better view of the fire engines.

She also had a better view of Nathan and his older brother, Garrett, standing in the headlights of one of the engines, deep in conversation.

She hadn't realized Nate was there, though it made perfect sense—his staff was probably so small that he had to report as well as edit—and she certainly hadn't realized that the deputy she'd spotted a few times on the fringes of the crowd was Garrett Marcenek. Go figure.

She'd known Garrett for years, and had no idea he'd ever thought of pursuing a career in law enforcement. How ironic. Now instead of being arrested, he'd get to do the honors. So what might Seth Marcenek be doing? If the rule of opposites applied, he'd pretty much have to be a priest.

"Hey, Garrett," someone behind her called. "I'm taking off."

The brothers both looked up, catching Callie midstare.

Damn.

She instantly started walking toward them, as if that had been her objective in the first place. If she was going to stay in this town for a while, then she wasn't going to try to avoid the Marcenek brothers.

"Garrett, good to see you," Callie said before either man could speak. She firmly believed that whoever spoke first had a psychological advantage. "Nathan."

"Callie." He revealed no emotion. No coldness, no warmth. Nothing.

"Welcome back," Garrett said, shifting his weight to his heels. Callie wondered if he was resting his hand on his holster on purpose, or if it was just a habit.

"Thank you."

"I need to check something out," Nathan said to his brother, his eyes focused behind Callie. He left without another word, brushing past a burly volunteer firefighter carrying a Pulaski ax. Nate favored one leg slightly, making Callie wonder just how many miles he was putting on the bike. Five to ten a day had been the norm when they'd been in high school, but he'd ride as many as twenty when he was stressed. She had gone with him on the short rides, but when he needed to put his head down and pedal, she'd found other things to do.

The man she'd seen unloading equipment from the minivan in the parking lot that morning was there, taking notes as he talked to one of the firefighters. He lowered his pad as Nathan approached, and the two fell into conversation. An old memory jarred loose. Chip Elroy. From her sophomore geometry class.

"So how long have you been a deputy?" Callie asked, turning back to Garrett.

"Since about a year after you dumped Nathan." He held her gaze, his expression cool and coplike.

"Eleven years then." She wasn't surprised by Garrett's response. The brothers had wildly different temperaments, with Garrett looking for trouble, Nathan trying to keep him out of it, but they were tight.

"Give or take a few months." He shifted his weight again. "What're you doing here?"

"You mean at the fire?" Obviously, since he had to know why she was back in Wesley. She glanced over at the trailer's smoldering metal ribs. "Just seeing if there's a story." She cocked her head. "Who's the female firefighter?"

"Denise Logan."

Ah, from high school. She would have been in Seth's graduating class.

"Was this arson?" When Garrett didn't respond, Callie added, "Pretty clear night. No lightning."

"How long are you staying in town?"

"Awhile."

"And then?"

She shrugged.

"Must be nice," Garrett replied, "having no ties. Going where you want, when you want."

"It's great," she agreed, refusing to rise to the bait. "You should try it."

"Can't. I prefer to be there for the people who matter to me."

"Oh, do you have some of those? People who matter to you? Because I remember you dumping girls right and left, without much regard for hurt feelings."

"At least I told them it was over, instead of taking the coward's way out and running away without a word."

She wasn't touching that one, and Garrett knew it.

He smiled without humor, then muttered, "I have some things I need to take care of." Nodding in dismissal, he strode past her toward two older men checking gauges on a truck.

Callie turned away and headed for the Neon. She got in without looking back, slamming the stubborn old door shut.

She fought the urge to rest her forehead on the steering wheel in defeat, and instead turned the key in the ignition, carefully pulling back out onto the road and then executing a three-point turn. She followed the route the kids had taken, to make sure they'd gotten home.

A few minutes later she turned down Grace's street and cruised by the house where the neighbor kids lived. It was dark inside, except for the distinctive glow of a television set, but the old bikes were propped against the porch. They were home. She debated stopping, but it was late, almost ten now. Maybe she'd try to catch the parents at home tomorrow and mention that the children had been at the fire. Parents who cared simply did not let kids ride across town—even a small town—after dark.

"So WHAT'S THE DEAL HERE?" Nathan asked, indicating the burned-out trailer with a jerk of his head. He'd rejoined his brother after he'd made certain that Chip, who'd thankfully put off his trip when he saw the smoke, would get his photos in before he left the next day. "Two fires in a week, no lightning."

Nathan hated fires. He hadn't had a problem until the explosion, when the world around him had erupted into a fireball. That was after the shock wave had thrown him back against a brick wall and driven shrapnel into his leg and torso. His partner, Suzanne Galliano, had also been injured, but her wounds had been superficial, which was why she was still reporting in Seattle, while he was back here in good old Wesley, Nevada.

"What do *you* think the deal is?" Garrett asked. He was careful what he said around Nathan in an official capacity, having been quoted as an "unnamed source" enough times to get him in trouble with the brass, who had no trouble figuring out the identity of the unnamed source.

Nathan rubbed a hand over his head, loosening his matted hair. "If it turns out this fire was man-made like the last one, then someone could be setting fires."

"That's a big leap, junior," Garrett said, careful not to be quotable. "A field and a structure."

"Or the fires may not be related and this one came about because old man Anderson wanted to get rid of his rusty trailer without paying to have it torn down and hauled away."

"Talk to Dad," Garrett said, jerking his head to where their father was conferring with another man near the front of an engine.

"Oh, I will. Later." Not that it would do a lot of good.

Fifteen years of being sheriff prior to taking over command of the fire department had made John Marcenek a master at avoiding a direct answer.

"My gut reaction is that the two incidents aren't connected, and you're probably right about Anderson," Garrett finally said, before giving Nathan a fierce look. "*Do not* quote me."

"Unnamed source," he agreed with a half smile. The brothers fell into step as they walked back to Nathan's car.

"Law enforcement officials are uncertain whether the incidents are connected," Garrett corrected. "You didn't seem too surprised to see Callie at the fire."

"Probably looking for a story. She showed up at the office and asked me for freelance work a couple days ago."

Garrett glanced at him. "No shit?"

"I turned her down, but if Vince Michaels hears about it, he'll be an unhappy camper."

"Or rather, you'll be an unhappy camper."

Nathan grinned for the first time all evening. "In your words, no shit."

As soon as Callie got home, she fired up her laptop and started to write. Words appeared on the screen, but something was lacking: decent writing. Disgusted, she ditched the file and turned off the computer. She'd try again tomorrow.

The next morning was no better, nor was the afternoon. Finally, as the sun was setting and Callie had accomplished nothing except for an industrial cleaning of the bathroom, she faced reality. She couldn't keep cleaning bathrooms and waxing floors. She had to do the one job she did not want to do, the task that was constantly lurking at the back of her mind, and then maybe she could settle and write a few words.

She needed to go through Grace's belongings.

Callie opened the bedroom door and stood in the doorway, taking in the neat little room. Grace's reading glasses were on the nightstand, along with an empty water glass, and a box of tissues set on top of a library book. Callie should probably return that before the library police came after her.

She went to the closet and opened the door, the squeak of the wheels in the tracks instantly bringing back memories. When the closet had squeaked, it meant Grace was awake, getting her robe. It meant Callie would smell breakfast soon and that the house would be warm when she got up.

The closet smelled of spice. Grace had loved cinnamon and had sachets everywhere. Callie had always loved cinnamon herself, but at the moment the scent was too poignant, too much.

Sorry, Grace…

Callie did her best to shut herself off as she pulled armloads of clothes out of the closet and laid them on the bed before going back for more. If she didn't think about what she was doing, she wouldn't get sucked down. And once she got this chore done, the worst would be behind her. She'd be able to write.

After the first closet was empty, she shook open a trash bag and shoved the clothing into it, hangers and all. If she stopped to sort and fold, she wouldn't make it through the process without breaking down. The most practical approach was to make everything disappear into black plastic as quickly as possible.

But Callie wasn't quick enough. She slowed down for a few seconds and the next thing she knew, she'd pulled an oversize cardigan she'd always associated with Grace out of the pile of clothing on the bed. And, instead of shoving it into the bag, she held it up, then bunched it to her, breathing in the scent of the only mother she'd ever really known.

Her throat closed.

Callie resolutely blanked her mind, folded the sweater and set it inside the swollen bag before tying it shut. She shook open another bag and headed for the dresser, planning to quickly sort through Grace's unmentionables so she didn't accidentally throw away or donate something of value. Grace had had a habit of hiding things in her underwear drawer, as if placing something here would keep it safe from prying eyes—those of a young girl trying to peek at her Christmas presents, for example. Sure enough, when Callie opened the drawer, something solid slid across the bottom. She pushed aside the cotton undergarments to find a fancy lingerie box.

She set the box on the bed and for a moment just looked at it, wondering what on earth it could contain that was worthy of hiding in the underwear drawer. The corners of the lid were worn and the cardboard had grown brittle with age. She gently eased the top off.

Photos. Tons of photos. And her schoolwork. Award certificates. Callie's life in a box.

She lifted out a photo of herself taken on the first day of junior high, wearing low-rider flared pants and a body-hugging, long-sleeved shirt. The shirt had been too hot for August in Nevada, but Callie had wanted to wear it, and Grace had acquiesced. Beneath that were more photos—showing her rabbit at the fair for 4-H. Callie riding her bike. Grace had bought it used, but it had been one of the cool bikes. A Trek 920, like Nathan's. Not that Callie had been concerned about that kind of stuff…. She smiled slightly. She'd pretended not to be, anyway, but she had loved having a bike that was as nice as everyone else's. Grace hadn't made a ton of money working at the grocery store, but she'd taken care of Callie.

Callie had not taken care of Grace.

She put the lid back on the box and set it on top of the dresser, then went back to the clothing, checking all the drawers before quickly dumping the contents into trash bags. No more sorting, because everything was going to charity. People who hadn't abandoned their foster mother could sift through her stuff.

By the time she finished, despite her best efforts to keep the self-recriminations at bay, Callie was a wreck.

She should have come home and she hadn't.

She'd shut everyone she'd ever been close to out of her life over the past decade, for reasons she didn't quite understand.

Well, damn it, she didn't want to be alone anymore.

CHAPTER FOUR

NATE WAS SLOUCHED on the sofa, his feet propped on the coffee table and his laptop on his thighs, when the dog next door started yapping. Since Poppy's owner went to bed at approximately sundown every night, Nate put his computer on the coffee table and went to the window to see what had disturbed the little rat.

"You've gotta be kidding me," he muttered as he dropped the curtain and went to the door. Callie was already on the bottom step when he pulled it open. Twice now he'd seen her and twice he'd felt the odd sensation of having a missing part of his life back again—which was ridiculous, since this missing part had blown him off and disappeared for a dozen years without a word.

"Why are you here?" It was late and he was too tired for niceties.

Her eyebrows lifted as she said, "Because I want to make peace."

He rested a hand against the door frame. "Make peace?" They weren't at war. He just didn't want her around.

"Over ten years have gone by, Nate. I'm sorry I took off, but we're different people now. Surely we can start new."

Start new. Yeah. So easy. He didn't feel like making it easy on Callie, so he continued to block the door, even though she obviously wanted to come inside.

"I went through hell after you left. I was afraid something had happened to you, until Grace told me you were all right." It had taken him a couple of days to get hold of her foster mother, since she'd traveled to Boise immediately after the graduation ceremony to attend a wedding, giving him and Callie the freedom to almost consummate their relationship, emphasis on *almost*. Her trip had also given Callie the freedom to blow town the next day.

His fingers gripped the door frame. He would never forget how he'd felt when he'd realized she'd gone without a word. He loved her, thought she'd loved him, yet she disappeared after their first awkward and unsuccessful attempt to make love. He'd felt like such a freaking loser.

"I did what I had to do," Callie said now, an edge of frustration creeping into her voice.

Nate ran a hand over the taut muscles at the back of his neck. "You didn't give a reason for leaving. So why don't you tell me now?"

"I don't know," she said softly.

For a moment he just stared at her. After all these years, this was her answer.

"'I don't know,'" he mimicked. "Bullshit!"

The word echoed through the night. Callie flinched, and he realized he'd never raised his voice to her. He drew in a ragged breath, leaning his forehead against the doorjamb. Callie was one of the most intelligent women he knew. Intelligent women didn't just abandon someone without a reason. And more than that, deep down he'd wanted her to have a concrete reason for leaving. Maybe something he'd done or said. Maybe his inexperience. Something they could have worked out, given a chance. He'd always believed she'd had a reason.

"We're not going to be friends and you're never writing for the *Star,* Callie. Not while I'm editor." He looked up at her. "Got it?"

She stared him down for a few seconds, then muttered something under her breath that sounded a whole lot like "We'll see," before she abruptly turned and crossed the lawn back to her wreck of a car. It started with a puff of blue smoke. She pulled away from the curb before she snapped the headlights on. Nathan watched her disappear around the corner.

What kind of a jerk treated someone who'd recently lost her only relative that way? Especially when he knew exactly how it felt to lose a parent?

But did Callie *ever* feel anything? He was really beginning to wonder.

THE NEON GAVE A COUPLE of ominous coughs as Callie drove home. Par for the course. Everything

else in her life was going to hell. Why not the borrowed car, too?

Nate was still angry with her. And he wanted answers
she didn't have.

Why had she left?

Why does a horse bolt at a loud noise? Instinct. It
was the way she was. She couldn't put a name to the
reason if she tried, since she didn't fully understand
it herself, but she did accept it. She panicked when
she felt as if she was being tied down, and according
to Grace, her father had been the same way. Hard to
fight genetics.

So what had made her think she could explain tonight? Or that after their first encounter in his office, that
Nate would listen? What had made her even try?

The need to be with someone who, even if he didn't
understand, might accept her as she was. After all, he
was Nate. He'd once loved her. She'd thought.

Callie bit her lip as she considered all the things she
should have said and hadn't, because she needed more
time to get them out.

She'd wanted to explain that he'd always been on her
mind after she'd left, that ending their relationship had
nearly ripped her apart, too, but the panic had been
stronger than her feelings for him. How could she get
that across to him?

She couldn't.

Yet.

But with time… With some time, maybe he'd come around. She missed him and she needed a friend.

When she got home, the Hobart house was still dark inside except for the flickering glow of the television. No car was parked in front of the house or in the carport.

Was someone home with those kids?

A television also glowed in Alice Krenshaw's living room, and there was no car parked in her drive, either, which was because Alice's husband worked the night shift at the mine and they owned only one vehicle. The Hobart family probably had the same circumstances. One car and shift work.

No matter how she twisted it around, though, it still bugged the heck out of Callie that those kids had been out so late without supervision. Twice.

Uncaring adult? Zero supervision? Or were the kids masters at sneaking out?

Was it any of her business?

And here she was, sitting in her car, spying on the house next door. How creepy was that? Callie got out of the little Neon, trying not to slam the stubborn door too loudly.

She'd left the lights on in Grace's house, but it looked anything but welcoming. Kind of a theme here in Wesley. Maybe that was the reason she hadn't come back sooner.

But deep down, she knew it wasn't.

CALLIE HAD DRIVEN AWAY half an hour ago and Nate was still keyed up, unable to focus for more than a few minutes, which was disturbing to a guy notorious for his ability to hyperfocus. He put the laptop aside and then absently ran his hand over the numb area of his thigh.

So what exactly did Callie want from him? Friendship? Forgiveness? Physical intimacy during a rough spot in her life? Perhaps all three. Who didn't want comfort when life took a devastating turn?

Him. Physical intimacy had been out of the question after the explosion nearly destroyed his leg. He'd had no desire to share his battered body, and even when he finally had, it had been with the woman who was his nurse during the latter part of his hospital stay, a woman who was accustomed to seeing trauma and injury. The relationship hadn't lasted long. Nate's heart hadn't been in it and he'd had a sneaking suspicion she was laying him just to get his confidence back up. He didn't need mercy screws.

Again he ran his hand over his leg, felt the twisted tissue and deep dip where the destroyed muscles had once been.

No. Even though he wouldn't mind showing Callie that he was no longer the inexperienced kid suffering from performance anxiety, there'd be no physical intimacy. He wasn't the guy to give her comfort, because he wasn't ready to put himself out there—especially with someone he couldn't trust.

In fact, it really pissed him off that she was back, acting as if nothing had happened, wanting to pick up where they'd left off before she'd abandoned him.

We're different people now, Nate.

In more ways than she knew.

Nathan got the laptop, settled it back onto his thighs and resolutely finished the article. He'd just shut the computer down and was ready to call it a night when his cell phone rang.

His leg had stiffened and it took a few minutes for it to cooperate as he crossed the room to the buffet table where the phone was plugged in, charging. He glanced at the number, expecting it to be one of his brothers, since it was so late, then smiled.

"Hey, Scoop." Suzanne Galliano had been his best friend in Seattle. They'd collaborated on several stories and had been together the night Nathan's investigation into the illegal import of pharmaceuticals ended in an explosion and warehouse fire. Fortunately for Suzanne, her hospital stay had been only two days, her recovery from the mostly superficial wounds rapid. Nate's recovery, on the other hand, not so much. Hell, in a lot of ways he'd yet to recover from the blast.

"Are you still stuck in the middle of nowhere?"

"You mean my charming hometown? Yeah. I'm here." He could almost see her rolling her eyes. "Well, maybe I'll be able to do something to save you. The paper just lost a reporter and they're hiring. You'd have to throw some stuff together fast, get it up here, but honestly, I think you have a good shot."

"No thanks."

"Nathan…!" she whined. "Come on. You know you don't belong where you are. You should be writing and reporting, not editing. I bet you'd make more money in this job than you do now, and it could be a springboard to bigger and better things."

"Thanks. I'll think about it."

"No you won't. I know that tone."

"I will. Honest."

She blew a raspberry into the receiver. "Fine. But you're throwing away an opportunity."

"I like being near family."

"The same members of your family who tried to kill you more than once as a child?"

"The very same," Nathan agreed as he shut off the living room lamp and walked into his bedroom. His brothers might have made a career out of attempting to do him bodily harm as a youngster, but he'd returned the favor. In spades. He might be the quiet brother, but he wasn't a wimp.

"You need to rethink your priorities, you masochist. If I don't hear from you by Wednesday, I'll assume it's a no and arrange for counseling."

"Thanks for the heads-up."

"No problem. I'll make you see the light one of these days. How's the *physical* therapy?"

Nathan smiled. "Over for the most part. I ride my bike. It keeps the leg strong and flexible." Plus, he'd been able to buy a bitchin' bike with the money he saved once the therapy stopped.

"There's some good bike riding here," Suzanne said in a sincere voice. "And I kind of miss you."

"I'll think about it. Hey, how's Julia?" Her significant other, who had never fully forgiven Nathan for dragging Suzanne down to the warehouse with him that fateful night.

"She's doing well. Just got a promotion to design manager."

"Tell her congratulations from me."

"Maybe you can tell her yourself when you come for the *interview*...." His ex-partner's voice trailed off hopefully.

"I'll think about it. Good night, Suze. Talk to you later."

Nathan tossed the phone onto the dresser and went into the bathroom, where he stared at himself in the mirror for a few seconds before turning on the water to brush his teeth.

It had been nothing short of a miracle when, after Nathan had returned to Wesley, Vince Michaels had bought the paper and promptly fired the editor. Newspaper jobs in a town the size of Wesley were nonexistent. Nathan lived near his dad and brothers, in the town he'd grown up in, doing the job he'd trained for. If he felt as if he was just going through the motions day to day, it was from the inherent stress of an editor's life. Survival mode.

He just needed to ride his bike more, take the edge off.

This was where he belonged.

CALLIE WOKE UP SHEATHED in sweat, the light cotton blanket that had covered her in a tangle at the end of the bed. She sat up, swung her feet onto the floor and then sat for a moment, her face in her hands.

Her heart was still hammering.

Crap. She'd thought she'd moved past the dream years ago.

She took slow, deep breaths until her heart rate slowed, then turned on the night table lamp and went to the bathroom. When she returned, she shook out the comforter and sheet, then lay back down. It was three-thirty. The dream never came twice in a night, so once her adrenaline level dropped, she might go back to sleep. Maybe.

It was unusual for the dream to come during such deep sleep. Usually it happened when she was nodding off, startling her fully awake, frightening her with…she had no idea what frightened her once the first images, recognizable in the split second when the dream struck, were forced back. A burning sensation in her nostrils, then terror would overwhelm her. Not shrieking, sheet-clutching terror, but a deeper fear that threatened to suffocate her. A feeling that she was going to be dragged into a dark unknown.

Over the years she'd learned not to panic, to breathe slowly through her nose, and the burning sensation, along with the terror, would pass. They already had now, leaving Callie to wonder, as always, what it was in this dream she would not allow herself to recall. What terrified her so much?

When she awoke again, sun was shining in through the window and the comforter was still covering her. No more dreams, no restless sleep.

Callie hated the dream, but she'd learned to live with it.

Now she wondered what had triggered it. She could usually link it to stress, but the greatest stress in her life—Grace's death—hadn't brought it on. So what was the cause tonight?

Nate. Had to be.

NATHAN WENT TO WORK and disappeared into his office, closing the door behind him. Between Callie's visit and Suzanne's call, he hadn't slept much, and he was not in the mood for socializing. Barely ten minutes passed before Joy was there with the boiled lettuce juice.

"I heard there was a bit of a scene at your house yesterday."

Nathan looked at her from beneath the hand that was propping up his head while he read.

"Yes," she continued, placing the cup on his desk near the dieffenbachia, "I talked to Ed Nelson at the café this morning and he said you were yelling at some good-looking woman on your lawn."

"I wasn't yelling." *Much,* he amended to himself, remembering how Callie had flinched when he'd shouted "bullshit." He'd had no idea that Ed, his neighbor across the street, had been listening.

Joy clasped her hands together over her shapeless navy blue dress. "Was it Callie you weren't yelling at?"

"Yes." He had the feeling from her body language that Joy had something to say on the matter, and out of curiosity, he waited, wondering if she was going to mention the fact that Callie had not come home to be with Grace when she was dying. But Joy didn't say anything.

Finally he gave in and asked, "You were a friend of Grace's. Did she ever mention anything about what happened between Callie and me at the end of high school?" *Do you understand that your normally sane employer had a reason for yelling at a woman on his front lawn?*

And had Callie gone with Grace's blessing? He'd never been able to figure it out the few times he'd talked to her after Callie had disappeared. Grace had simply assured him that her niece was fine, and had obviously wanted him to let the matter rest.

He'd been so frustrated. Callie was safe, but for reasons unknown, did not want to talk to him. His brothers were the only people he'd ever spoken to concerning the matter, and he hadn't said much. Since he'd left town himself for a summer job shortly after graduation, and went on to college in the fall, he figured no one cared what had happened. So what if nerdy Nathan Marcenek had been blitzed by tornado Callie? But Wesley was a small town and gossiping was a hobby for some.

Joy contemplated him as if looking for signs of a hangover. "I vaguely remember people wondering why she took off like she did." She shifted her mouth sideways in a thoughtful manner. "And it was kind of obvious a few days ago that you didn't want her back in your life."

He really was going to have to remember to close the office door.

"So Grace never said anything?" He felt ridiculously like an insecure teenager as he asked the question.

"Grace was protective of Callie," Joy said after a tactful pause.

"That didn't work in the other direction, did it?" he asked darkly, truthfully. Callie hadn't been protective of Grace.

"No." Joy shook her head, the fluorescent light glinting on the few strands of gray in her black hair. "It didn't."

The phone rang, and ironically, Joy, who'd planted herself in his office without invitation, appeared relieved to have a reason to escape. He didn't blame her. "Do you want me to close the door?"

"Please."

A moment later, she sent him an e-mail, apparently not wanting to risk a continuation of their previous conversation. Mitch Michaels would be showing up for his first day of work next Monday. Did he want her to reschedule Katie's office hours so they didn't coincide?

Nathan considered it. Then he came up with a better idea. He wrote a quick reply, telling Joy to leave Katie's hours as they were. Mitch would be working in the basement on the archives. The kid wouldn't see the light of day while he was in the office. Vince might be able to force Nathan to babysit his son and try to teach him a work ethic, but he didn't have much say in what the kid actually did.

SINCE CALLIE ALWAYS FELT unsettled and basically rotten the morning after the dream, it seemed a perfect time to dive into Grace's personal files. The accountant had phoned the day before and had reported the estate was all but settled, so now it was up to Callie to finish her end of the deal so that she could move on.

She soon came to realize, though, that no time was perfect for diving into personal files. Grace had kept everything, from the warranty on her new kitchen faucet to the property deed, in a tall, wooden, three-drawer file cabinet. Callie sorted for two hours, keeping the documentation that would be handy to the new owners of the home, tossing paperwork on items that were long gone.

In the back of drawer number two, she found a file with her name on it. Even though it held the paperwork on the foster care arrangements, this was much less distressing to her than finding her schoolwork and certificates in the old lingerie box in Grace's dresser had been.

The folder contained duplicate immunization records, her high school transcripts and SAT scores, among other things. She glanced over the foster care papers, then closed the folder and stashed it in the box she was putting in storage back in California. Someday. She wasn't sure when. It was going to take some time to go through the house single-handedly, and she was going to take that time. She needed it, to make peace with herself for not being there when Grace needed her.

She finished the third and final file drawer just before noon. She had a giant bag of paper to be shredded or burned, and a giant headache. Time for iced tea and a peanut butter sandwich, even though it felt as if a stiff belt of vodka would come closer to hitting the spot.

She dragged one of the wicker porch chairs out into the tall grass under the elm tree and ate in the shade. It was hot, but she wanted to be out of the house, away from the memories.

The kids next door were playing in the vacant lot that separated their houses. Callie could hear them arguing about who was pitching and who was hitting, and wondered if a ball would soon come sailing over her fence, perhaps followed by a white-haired kid.

She clinked the ice in her glass. The grass desperately needed to be cut. She'd put the job off twice because she hadn't wanted to tackle the mower. Although she'd done well with her tire store job, she was not the most mechanically inclined person, and was fairly certain the mower would win if it came down to a battle of wills. When she'd been a teen, Grace had beaten the mechanical monster into submission, somehow managing to get it started every weekend so that Callie could mow the lawn and earn her allowance. Now she was on her own.

In this corner, Callie McCarran, and in the other, Lawn-Boy...

But maybe Grace had a new mower. Callie got out of the wicker chair and walked to the shed, flipping open the latch with a quick movement of her thumb. It took a moment for her eyes to adjust, but as soon as they did, she recognized her old opponent lurking in the far corner.

Okay. Maybe she'd hire a kid to do the job—one with his own mower.

Feeling better about the lawn situation, she was about to close the door when she suddenly recognized the weirdly shaped dusty object with garden tools leaning against it. Her old bike, her once beautiful Trek, with a coil of hose hanging off the handlebars. Callie swung the door open wider and stepped inside, amazed that Grace hadn't donated the bike to charity years ago, and ridiculously happy that she hadn't. Callie removed the hose and laid it on the useless lawn mower, gathered the rake, hoe and shovel and jammed them into the corner.

After a quick spider check, she wiped the cobwebs off and lifted the bike, coughing as she accidentally inhaled some of the dust that had settled on the frame. She hauled the Trek out of the shed and laid it on the lawn, then turned the hose on it. Years of dirt and spiderwebs washed into the grass and disappeared.

Her baby was a wreck.

The tires were flat, the chrome pitted and the seat cracked. The chain hung sadly. She found the hand pump in the shed under the tool bench and tried to put air in the tires, but it was no use. The inner tubes were goners, having endured extreme temperature changes over the past decade. Callie propped the bike against the shed door and considered what she'd have to do to make it operational. Everything. A complete overhaul and tune-up were in order, but for the moment new tubes and tires and an oiled chain would probably suffice.

She'd never been a cycling maniac like Nathan and his brothers, but she'd loved her bike and had enjoyed getting from point A to point B under her own steam. She still liked the idea, and with the Neon acting up, an alternate mode of transportation was quite possibly a godsend.

And maybe a way to connect with Nate, because damn it, she wasn't giving up. Her old friend was in there somewhere, and truthfully, the man he had become was very, very attractive. He also appeared to be lonely, and if he would just listen to reason, he and Callie could solve both problems at once.

CHAPTER FIVE

"IT'S YOUR TURN TO FORCE Dad to go to the doctor," Garrett said over the phone in his commanding cop voice.

Nathan was not one bit impressed. "I'm behind schedule," he answered, changing computer screens to pull up his calendar. "And it's not my turn."

"It is, too, and you're always behind schedule."

"The news never stops."

"Come on, Nate. You're better at this than I am."

"You're a cop. Coercion is part of your business. Anyway, it's Seth's turn."

"Hey…" Nathan could hear his brother flipping through his desk calendar. "You're right. It's your turn in October."

"Can't wait," Nathan said drily. His other line lit up. "Gotta go. Call me if you need backup."

"I can't imagine not," Garrett said succinctly before hanging up.

John Marcenek had had no problems with doctors until he started having health issues related to high blood pressure, which culminated in a ministroke that he sneeringly called "the episode." After that, he developed a strong dislike of those in the medical profession—especially those who told him to stop drinking and lose weight if he wanted to avoid future "episodes."

The truth was hard to handle, especially when it involved changing a lifestyle filled with manly habits such as eating bags of chips and pork rinds during the televised game and drinking too much. He'd left law enforcement after more than thirty years—fifteen spent as county sheriff—when he hit the mandatory retirement age. After that he poured his energy into being chief of the volunteer fire department. John Marcenek was accustomed to command and didn't take well to being ordered around. Even for his own health and well-being. Garrett and Seth were very much like the old man, with he-man occupations John approved of and he-man hobbies. Nathan had always been the odd man out—the son his father didn't understand. The son who wrote and drew. Because of that, Nathan actually was the best candidate to strong-arm his father to the clinic. Since they had never seen eye to eye, he was used to his dad's bellowing, and took it in stride. If he hadn't developed that ability, he would have imploded long ago.

The only time he'd seen a different side to his father was after his accident. John had hovered uncomfortably near his bedside in Seattle, while Seth and Garrett held down the fort in Wesley. His dad hadn't said much about the injury itself, talking instead about sports and stuff, but after that Nathan was convinced his dad loved him in his own way. John would never understand his middle son, and wasn't going to try and Nathan had learned to accept that.

CALLIE CLOSED HER LAPTOP and pressed her fingertips against her forehead. She'd been back for three weeks, had sorted through all of Grace's belongings. The estate was settled and still…nothing. No words. She would start writing, then suddenly feel the need to wash walls, sort out stuff in the basement, escape the keyboard.

Her last finished piece had been the Kazakhstan article, written after her trip had abruptly ended, when she'd gotten word of Grace's death. Callie had composed the contracted article in a numb haze. She'd written in airports and hotel rooms on her fractured journey here, since getting a quick flight home from central Asia wasn't exactly a piece of cake. She'd been practically finished by the time she'd gotten to the States, did the last editing the night before leasing the Neon from the friend of the friend to drive to Wesley, and had submitted by e-mail.

She couldn't remember a word she had written. She didn't know if what she'd sent in was a piece of crap or up to her usual standards, and she hadn't been able to bring herself to open the file on her computer, for fear of what she might find. So when the check arrived in the mail, forwarded from her San Francisco post office box, she decided the piece must have been adequate, because the payment was unusually rapid.

Now she had some money to tide her over until she received her substitute teaching license or Mrs. Copeland called from Tech Temps. Callie was hoping for the latter. She still wasn't certain how she felt about subbing, but what concerned her more was the lack of spark in her writing. Something had to change. Or else she was going to have to change her occupation, perhaps even take up something permanently.

Callie didn't want to do that. She needed the freedom to get up and go when she felt the urge.

She did have an idea niggling at her that she thought would make a very nice submission to the *Wesley Star.* Maybe she'd write it, submit and see how Nathan reacted. Perhaps now that he'd vented the frustrations he'd had bottled up for ten years, he'd be more reasonable.

Callie certainly hoped so, because that was an integral part of her plan.

It wasn't difficult to hunt down Denise Logan, the female firefighter. Callie asked about her in the grocery store, and the clerk, not knowing that Callie was a horrible person who had abandoned her foster mom, told her a few things about the woman. Like where she lived. With that information Callie was able to dig up Denise's phone number and arrange a coffee and an interview at the new café.

Callie was waiting in a red upholstered booth when Denise came in at exactly two-thirty—a time when the place was nearly empty, and they could talk and not worry about taking up a table. Denise smiled and raised a hand when she spotted Callie. Her long blond hair was pulled back in a ponytail and she was wearing almost exactly the same outfit as Callie—a formfitting T-shirt, denim skirt and leather sandals. She looked nothing like the all-business firefighter Callie had seen the previous week.

"Thanks for coming," Callie said as Denise slid into the booth.

"Hey, thanks for asking me. I've never been interviewed before." Denise waved help at the waitress who came out from behind the counter. They ordered iced tea, and then Denise settled back in her seat and waited for the questions to begin.

Callie pulled out her small tape recorder. "Do you mind if I record your answers?"

"Not at all."

"You grew up around here," Callie said. She remembered the Logan kids, all several years younger than herself. The junior and senior high schools were combined. "Did you always plan to stay in Wesley?"

"Oh, no," Denise said with an easy smile. "I went to the University of Nevada, Reno, got my degree in fire science at their school near Carlin. But—" Denise held up her palms, her expression philosophical "—there are no jobs, so I moved home."

"Why did you get a degree in a field where there are no jobs?"

Denise's eyes brightened. "Because when there is a job opening, I'm going to get it."

Callie laughed. "I like the way you think. How do you support yourself while you wait for that job?"

"I'm a bookkeeper at the junior and senior high."

"And they give you time off when you get a fire call?"

"That's one reason I work there."

"Are there other reasons?"

"Well, the hours are good. I work from seven to two. Also—" she smiled ironically before sipping her iced tea "—I didn't have a lot of choice. The school district is one of the main employers in the county. If there's a non-mining-related job to be had, there's a good chance it's at one of the schools."

"That's what I discovered," Callie said, then told the story of her own search for a temp job.

"So you *only* work temp?" Denise seemed surprised.

"I've never been on a job for longer than six months."

"Wow. I don't know whether to be impressed or appalled," the blonde said candidly.

"Working temp allows me to write for a living. Travel. Fun stuff like that."

"Sounds cool, actually, so I guess I'll go with being impressed. I subbed for a while before I got the book-keeping position."

"What's substitute teaching like?" Callie felt compelled to ask the question, hoping for a reassuring answer.

"Like holding thirty corks underwater." Denise laughed at Callie's horrified expression. "Sorry," she said with a shrug. "But it's true. Be prepared to be busy."

"Tell me about fire school." Callie changed the subject back to research, and made a mental note to pop in and see Mrs. Copeland at Tech Temps on the way home.

"It's rigorous, but so worthwhile…." Denise answered questions for almost twenty minutes before the café door swung open and a group of high school boys traipsed in, laughing and pushing one another, obviously glad to have made it through the school day. Thankfully, they settled at a table across the room from Callie and Denise, but one kid smiled at Denise in a confident and blatantly wolfish way before turning his attention back to his buddies. Callie was amazed at the balls of the kid. Denise worked at his school and should command a degree of respect rather than the once-over he'd just given her.

"Tyler Michaels," Denise said, sipping her iced tea. "He lives on the hill above my house and his dad owns the newspaper and some other businesses."

"He's confident," Callie said, her eyes on the boys, who were now teasing the waitress.

"You should see his brother, Mitch. Unfortunately,

they have looks, lots of money, no respect, and they think they're God's gift to women."

"That kid must be all of fourteen. Kind of young to be God's gift to women."

"Fifteen. Doesn't slow him down one bit. And Mitch is even worse. I had to smack Mitch down at the school and now I guess his little brother is taking a shot."

How nice. Denise's carefree attitude had evaporated as soon as the teens arrived, so Callie decided to wrap things up.

"One last question." The most important one. "How does the old guard feel about a young female firefighter with a college degree joining the ranks?" *How is it working for that ass, John Marcenek?* Callie couldn't count the number of times she'd tried to talk to him and had gotten gruff put-downs for her efforts. It was as if she wasn't good enough for Nate, or had been somehow leading him astray.

Denise rolled her eyes. "Where do I begin?"

"At the beginning?"

She hesitated, then leaned forward, placed her palms on the table and said seriously, "Before I answer, promise me you won't write anything that will get me in trouble with the guys I work with."

"I'll be tactful."

"Well, let's just say it was a while before they took me seriously."

"In other words, you had to prove yourself."

"Yeah," Denise said, relaxing against the red booth cushion, her smile returning. "If you put it that way, it sounds all right."

"How long did it take…?"

When Callie left the restaurant, she felt confident that her writing slump was over. She was already composing the article in her head, had her lead, so the question now was how was she going to sell this article when the editor of the local paper had told her in no uncertain terms that he wouldn't publish anything she wrote?

That was a toughie.

Callie unlocked the Neon, pausing to watch the teens leave the café and pile into a car parked on the other side of the lot, before climbing into the stiflingly hot interior and rolling down the window to let some marginally cooler air circulate inside. The kids drove by and Callie glanced over in time to see Tyler Michaels smile at her. The kid did think he was something.

Callie wondered if the dad, the owner of the paper, was the same way. She would soon find out.

On a hunch, she returned to the small grocery store where she'd found out how to track down Denise. As she had hoped, the same bored clerk was behind the register. Callie picked up a few items and set them on the counter. As the young woman started scanning the bar codes, Callie asked in a conversational tone where she might find Vince Michaels. The clerk glanced up. After explaining exactly where Vince Michaels lived—

this clerk was truly a stalker's dream—Callie asked if he could be found anywhere in town. Like, in an office.

No office, but he played golf.

Interesting. Especially to a woman who for one entire season was the worst player on the Wesley High School girls' golf team.

JOY TAPPED ON THE DOOR and came in with the tea. Nathan had already dumped one cup that day, so he frowned at the second.

"Callie's here."

A day full of surprises. It made him wonder what kind of magic the evening might bring. "Send her in," he said with a sigh of resignation.

She paused in his office doorway a few seconds later, looking wonderful. He hated that she looked wonderful, hated that he still reacted to her.

"Good to see you, Callie."

She stretched her lips into a humorless smile. "Gee. With a little practice, you could sound like you mean that."

"I'll work on it," he said drily.

"I ran into Vince Michaels on the golf course."

Instant headache. "*You* were playing golf," Nathan said flatly. Callie was awful at golf. She'd all but been kicked off the girls' team the one year she'd played.

"I was practicing my swing with my old clubs, hitting a bucket of balls the same time he was."

"How'd you manage that?"

"I'm not without resources."

Yeah. Nate imagined that Jesse Martinez, the golf pro, would have provided a wealth of information if approached in a proper manner. By an attractive female.

"Shouldn't you be mourning Grace instead of playing golf?"

"I am mourning Grace," Callie said in an intense voice.

Nathan felt a twinge of guilt at the low blow, but still—sucking up to his boss? He hadn't seen that one coming.

"Anyway, I mentioned this great idea I had of writing a series of articles while I'm here. Unique career choices in a small town. Doll maker. Lady firefighter. Geriatric kindergarten teacher. He seemed quite interested. He's heard of my work, you know." Callie idly fingered the fabric of her blouse. "Of course, the final decision is up to you."

"And we both know what that decision will be."

"Look, Nate." Her chin jutted out. "I was with you after your mom passed away. I admit I had no idea what you were going through until now, and you didn't talk much, but I was there. I'm just asking you to return the favor."

"You're blackmailing me into being your friend?"

"I'm blackmailing you into letting me write for you, and if I really need to, to talk to you. Friendship will come later."

"That ship sailed."

"Nothing's saying it can't come back to port."

"I'm saying."

"Okay, we'll hold off on the friendship clause. What about the articles?"

She spoke offhandedly, but Nathan was probably one of the few people on earth who was aware that Callie hid her vulnerabilities that way. She was hurting.

He'd been dead honest when he'd said they wouldn't be friends again, because friendship involved trust. He no longer trusted Callie, but he felt for her. He couldn't help it, having lost his own mother.

He gritted his teeth as if trying to hold back the words he knew were coming.

"Write one article on spec."

She didn't exactly break out smiles, but she seemed satisfied with the small concession.

"And the other…?"

"I'll listen if you need someone to talk to," he replied gruffly. But that was all he was going to do, and only because he owed her. "Once or twice. Plan accordingly."

"Another thing."

"There's more? What do you want? My car?"

"You're close. Can you give me the name of a decent auto mechanic in town?"

"I go to R&M."

"How about bikes?"

Nathan frowned.

"I found my old bike," she explained. "It needs a tune-up and new tires."

"Elko."

"The Neon won't make it to Elko and the bike is my transportation while the Neon's in the shop."

"Bring it over to my place. I'll see what I can do." He leaned back in his chair, folding his arms over his chest.

"Tonight?"

"Tomorrow around six. What size rims? Twenty-six?"

"I don't know."

"Measure them when you get home. If they're not twenty-six inch, call me."

"Great. See you then." She turned, looking so happy that Nathan almost hated to ruin the moment. But he did.

"This is a one-time deal, Cal. I'll help you out because of circumstances." His mouth tightened before he added, "Because I owe you for being with me after Mom died. But you owe me, too."

She was no longer smiling. "What do you want me to do about it?"

"Nothing. And I mean that from the bottom of my heart."

THE HOBART BOY DASHED across the empty lot to his house just as Callie turned onto their street. It was dark. The library had just closed and she was on her way home with a folder of research on unusual occupations people had held in Wesley over the years, gleaned from the special collections. So what was the kid doing out at nine o'clock again? Alone this time.

What disturbed her most was that the Hobart house was once again dark. This time there wasn't even the glow of a television showing through the windows.

Was that kid in there sitting in the dark? Surely if an adult were home, the house wouldn't be pitch-black.

Callie forgot all about minding her own business and marched up to the front door and knocked. No answer. She knocked again. Nothing.

So now what? Was she nuts? Did she or did she not see a white-haired kid? Was he inside or hiding in the thick foliage that surrounded the house?

Slowly, she walked down the buckling sidewalk toward her own house, then on impulse walked past her gate to Alice's.

Her neighbor answered on the first knock. "Hello, Callie," she said stiffly.

"Hi. I, uh…" She pointed down the street. "Do you know if there's an adult home at the Hobarts'?"

"There must be."

"No one answered when I knocked and there's no car."

"It looks dark," Alice said helpfully. "Maybe they aren't home."

"I saw the boy go into the house." Or at least she thought she had.

"Oh, my. Well, Callie, I don't know what to tell you.

The mom works downtown at the Winners Casino, but…" Alice's plump face brightened. "I think her mother lives with them. Yes. I seem to remember hearing that at club."

"Well, if she's there, she's fond of the dark."

Alice cocked her head, then stepped out onto the porch to look at the Hobart house. "Maybe the electricity got turned off. That does happen, you know. And I don't believe the family is well off financially. Single mom working at a casino…" She shook her head.

Callie moistened her lips thoughtfully. "So you think everything is all right?"

"I think I wouldn't go sticking my nose in their business. They can be a cantankerous bunch."

"Didn't they just move here?"

"From the Bellow's Ridge area. The family has been up there for generations." Bellow's Ridge was an extremely rural ranching community forty miles from Wesley.

"I see." Callie nodded as she digested the information, then attempted a smile, even though she wasn't reassured. The smile must have come off as genuine, though, because Alice smiled back. "Thanks," Callie said.

"You bet. Good night, Callie." Alice started closing the door, then stopped and asked, "How long do you plan on staying?"

"I don't know," she said truthfully.

Alice's fingers tightened on the half-open door. "Why didn't you come home when Grace was sick?"

Callie's shoulders rose and fell as she inhaled, then exhaled. "Poor planning on my part," she finally answered. "Good night, Alice."

Callie stayed up past midnight, reading, jotting notes, staring into space.

Every now and then she would go to her side window and look out at the Hobarts'. It was still dark. No television glow. Nothing. That bothered Callie immensely.

She thought about calling the police, but…what if she didn't have her facts right? What if she'd strung a bunch of minor incidents together and come up with a scenario that was blown all out of proportion because of her own experience having a working parent—not that her father had neglected her. He'd always seen that she was cared for.

Callie was still not certain what her dad had done for a living, why he'd traveled so much. She'd been very young when she'd been with him, and he couldn't exactly take her on the road with him—especially after she'd entered kindergarten and then first grade. She had few clear memories of who she'd stayed with, for how long or why, but she recalled being with many different people. She'd even stayed with Grace a time or two before that fateful trip when her father had dropped her off, never to return.

She'd asked Grace what her father had done for a

living exactly twice. The first time she'd been in elementary school and had been curious, since all the other kids were spouting off about what work their dads did. Grace had told her he was a traveling salesman. Years later, Callie had asked again, thinking that "traveling salesman" might have been a euphemism Grace had used for a seedier occupation—such as drug dealer or something. But the answer had been the same.

Callie had pushed a little more, asking if he was involved in any kind of criminal activity that may have gotten him killed. Grace had replied that to the best of her knowledge, Callie's father had been a salesman or unemployed, as finances allowed. And he'd loved traveling. No. He'd needed to travel.

Callie understood the need to travel, and because of what Grace had told her, knew that she came by her inability to settle in one place honestly. Yet…here she was in Wesley, where she had been ensconced in Grace's house for a couple weeks now, and she hadn't yet felt the tug to move on, to see what was around the next curve in the road.

The tug would come.

It always did.

CHAPTER SIX

MITCH MICHAELS WAS well dressed and personable, a kid meant to manage—as long as it didn't take a lot of effort on his part. Nathan was willing to concede that maybe Mitch would be all right if he was doing something he actually wanted to do. And there were no women around. Truthfully, Nate despised the kid and resented being saddled with him at the paper. He didn't have a much higher opinion of Mitch's younger brother, Tyler, who thankfully was not yet an intern. That day was coming, though. Nathan was certain of it.

"Hey, Mitch," he said when the young man swaggered into his office later that day. "Have a good summer?"

"It was all right." Once upon a time, the statement would have been accompanied by a charming smile. Not anymore. Not since Nathan had set Mitch straight on the matter of sexual harassment last spring. "It was nice to get out of this hellhole town for a while."

Mitch and Tyler had been urban transplants five years ago, when Vince had moved to Wesley from Salt Lake City after his divorce, and built a mansion in the foothills of the Jessup Mountains. He wanted his sons to grow up in a less complicated environment, he'd said, but Nathan suspected that he wanted to get his boys as far away from his flaky ex-wife as possible.

Whatever the reason, Mitch was being groomed to follow in his father's footsteps and take over either the newspapers or the trailer manufacturing business Vince was developing near Elko.

Last spring Nathan had had the kid answering phones and doing office work, which had proved to be a disaster. It ended in Nathan's explanation to Mitch that if the kid persisted in harassing Katie, Nathan would personally make sure she pressed charges.

"My dad wouldn't like that." Mitch had worn an expression that made Nathan want to smack him, which was what the kid had probably been angling for.

Nathan had merely shaken his head, unfazed. "Your dad has nothing to do with it. What you're doing is illegal."

Mitch had shown no sign of believing Nathan. But it was possible that he'd discussed the matter with his father later, because for the last three weeks of the internship, he'd shown up, sullen and withdrawn, and had kept to himself, doing the smallest amount of actual work possible and making everyone feel uncomfortable while he was there.

When the school year ended and he headed off for the summer with his mother, Nathan didn't know who was happier, Mitch, Katie or himself.

And now Mitch was back, but this time he was going to be where nobody had to deal with him—in the basement, scanning and digitalizing the archives, thus killing two birds with one stone. Vince had purchased the equipment the previous year, but no one in the office had time to do it. Perfect solution for everyone.

Nathan explained to Mitch what he'd be doing while the kid stared back at him stonily. "Do you understand?" Nate finally asked.

"Yeah."

"Chip's already down there printing photos. He'll show you how to run the equipment and then you're on your own."

Nathan watched Mitch descend the basement steps with the air of someone who was going to have to do something about this situation. Though he understood very well why Vince wanted Mitch to work, Nathan truly wished he wasn't the lucky guy in charge of transforming Prince Mitch into a hardworking employee.

Mitch paused three steps down and looked back. "This'll be my only job this semester?"

"Yeah."

"I'll sure learn a lot about running a paper," he said snidely.

"You want to run a paper, Mitch?" Nate had heard that the kid actually wanted to be a doctor, probably for the prestige and the money.

"Not really."

"Then I guess this'll work for both of us."

As soon as Mitch had disappeared, he returned to his office. He'd barely brought up the screen when Joy came in with a typed article in one hand.

"Callie McCarran just dropped this by. You might want to take a look," she said in a tone indicating she was aware of the possibility that he wouldn't. "It's pretty good."

Nathan gazed at her over his glasses. Joy held the article out. "Read it."

He leaned back in his chair and did as she asked, reading Callie's take on Denise Logan. It was well crafted, but he expected nothing less from Callie. She'd caught the essence of what it was like to be a formally trained, young female firefighter on a volunteer crew of older men. He knew for a fact that his father, as fire chief, had given Denise fits and she had done the same to him.

"Good article," he agreed. His dad was going to hate it.

"You're going to reject it."

"No." He tossed the article onto a side table and went back to his computer. Joy stood where she was for a long moment, but when he refused to look up, she finally retreated.

THE PHONE RANG at 6:30 A.M. It had to be a wrong number. Callie had lain awake deep into the night and had finally fallen asleep sometime in the early hours of the morning. The last thing she needed was some jerk who couldn't dial right waking her up. She grabbed the phone to stop the ringing, rolling over onto her back as she said hello in a voice that sounded as if she'd been out carousing for most of the night.

"Miss McCarran?"

Callie's eyes popped open. Not a wrong number. "Yes?"

"This is Nelda Serrano from Wesley High. Would you be available to sub today?"

"I…uh…don't think I have the license yet."

"It came into the district office yesterday. Your personal copy should arrive soon."

"Okay. Sure." This was what she'd signed on for. "What time do I get there?"

"You'll be subbing for Mr. Lightfoot, one of our English teachers, and you'll need to be here no later than seven forty-five. Come to the office when you arrive."

"Will do. Bye."

Callie got out of bed and went into the bathroom, squinting at herself in the mirror. Was this really a good idea?

It was a paycheck and she wouldn't mind one of those. Besides, as a serial temp, she was used to jumping in and fearlessly doing jobs with which she had only a passing familiarity. She couldn't remember a job, though, that caused her such anxiety prior to arriving on-site. Usually she needed to see equipment she had no idea how to run—state-of-the-art copy machines and such—before she felt any real anxiety.

It was the kids.

What did she know about handling kids? And it didn't help matters when she recalled classes during her own school days where the sub had been rather viciously terrorized. Had she taken part in those attacks? She certainly hoped not, but her memory was hazy. She did remember enjoying the spectacle...*oy*.

What had those subs done to provoke attack? she mused as she brushed her teeth. They'd shown vulnerability. Callie wouldn't do that. No vulnerability.

An hour after the call, Callie parked the sputtering Neon in the faculty lot, hoping she qualified, and walked through the nearly empty halls to the office. Mrs. Serrano was waiting for her.

"Thank goodness. If you hadn't been available, then the principal would have had to cover the class, which would have put me in charge of entertaining the discipline cases until he got back to the office."

"You don't like being the hammer?" Callie asked as she accepted a stack of papers from Mrs. Serrano.

"Not one bit." The woman took a set of keys out of a metal cabinet and handed them to Callie. "You turn these in before you go home. Dismissal time for teachers is three-thirty."

"Got it."

"I'll introduce you to some teachers in the neighboring rooms who can help you out. You went to school with Tanya Munro, I think, and your neighbor across the hall is Dane Gerard. The kids call him Great Dane." Callie was curious to see what a guy called Great Dane looked like.

They stopped at a door around the corner and down the hall from the office—the room where Callie had had history class back in the day. Mrs. Serrano let Callie open the door, perhaps testing to see if she could manage, because the old lock was a touch sticky. Callie prevailed and entered the room.

Chaos. There were messy stacks of paper on every available surface. Piles of books. Old newspapers. Contents of the basket marked Turn In were heaped almost as tall as Callie, it seemed.

"Mr. Lightfoot is one of our more free-form teachers."

"I, uh, can see that." Callie started toward the desk that would be her home base for the remainder of the day.

"And, well…" She turned back to see Mrs. Serrano still hovering near the door, as though she wanted to get away quickly after delivering more bad news. "I'm not sure there's a lesson plan."

Callie's eyes must have filled half of her face. A step-by-step plan was an absolute necessity. "I…" She couldn't back out now. Could she? She might be able to push past Mrs. Serrano and outrun her down the hall….

"No worries," the woman said quickly. "All the teachers have contingency plans in their file cabinet in case of unexpected absences such as this."

"Was there an emergency?"

"Just a touch of the flu." Callie got the feeling that Mrs. Serrano wasn't buying Mr. Lightfoot's story. "He plans to be back tomorrow."

"Is it normal not to have a lesson plan?"

Mrs. Serrano let out a telling sigh. "It is for Mr. Lightfoot, but in general, no. Why don't you just…" she sucked in a breath through her teeth "…check the top file drawer. There should be a red folder in there."

Callie could almost hear the woman's silent plea *Please be there, please be there* as she slid the drawer open. The red folder was there. Callie pulled it out, held it up. The secretary let out a sigh, then walked across the room to the cluttered desk.

"Wonderful. Now here's the lesson-plan book." Mrs. Serrano pulled a light green binder out from under a stack of creative-writing journals on the corner of the desk. "And there's the grade book. Take attendance in that. The symbols are marked in the front." The secretary's head jerked up as the phone in the office started ringing. "I need to get back to the phones. Tanya and Dane aren't here yet, but when they do arrive—"

"I'll introduce myself. Thanks, Mrs. Serrano."

A moment later, the secretary was gone. Callie opened the red folder. It contained word search puzzles.

Okay. So far so good. She checked the lesson plan book and found the pages were blank for that week. Not so good. The grade book thankfully had names written in it, but no seating charts. She remembered hating them as a student, but right now they seemed like a very good idea. No luck.

Callie sat down behind the messy desk. She had no idea what grade she was teaching, but she had word searches, a grade book with names in it and the will to survive. What more did she need?

Dane Gerard, a tall man with sandy hair and a handsome face, leaned in the door to introduce himself. When he saw Callie he came on into the room. Callie was familiar with the drill. Small town, new single woman.

"Do you need help with anything?" he asked, shaking his head in commiseration as he surveyed the room.

"What grade am I teaching?"

His blue eyes came back to her. "Sophomores. They're harmless."

Harmless to him maybe. He was used to them.

"How about seating charts?"

"Phillip doesn't believe in them."

Good for Phillip. "Any helpful hints?" She was certain she'd have many questions as soon as the school day started, but she didn't know the specifics yet.

"Watch your back?"

Callie smiled in spite of herself. "Thanks."

"Just take attendance using these slips," he held up a pad that had been sitting on the podium, "hand out the word-search puzzles and watch them work. That's all you have to do." There was a glint in his eyes as he said "It'll be fine. Honest. The first time is the hardest, but once you get to know the kids, it's a snap."

"I have no choice but to believe you." She leaned back against the white board, determined to relax. "So what do you do around here?"

Dane settled a hip on the desk and explained that he coached both boys' and girls' basketball and used to be a player himself. Now he taught algebra and calculus. He was also quite full of himself, but considering the circumstances, Callie thought it best to disregard that. She might need him soon.

The bell rang and Callie jumped. Dane pushed off from the desk.

"Give a yell if you need help," he said as he crossed the classroom. The first student came in the door just as Dane went out. "Ready or not, here they come."

"Or not," Callie muttered to herself.

She went to stand by the door because it seemed like the thing to do. The students continued to file into the room, eyeing her as if taking her measure. Callie was careful not to appear perky or enthusiastic, which she remembered as being sub-attack triggers. Instead she did her best to radiate quiet confidence.

Almost all of the boys were taller than she was and

the majority of the girls better dressed. Callie's yellow camp shirt and denim skirt seemed bland next to heeled ankle boots, skinny jeans and tops that in many cases were cut just a wee bit low. And everybody smelled good. She'd forgotten the maintenance that went into high school.

"Are you a sub?" a boy with two lip piercings asked as he sauntered past without waiting for an answer.

"You're new," commented a girl with a stylishly draped scarf who plopped down in the desk next to the door. She inspected Callie's outfit as if she were Heidi Klum judging a runway contest.

"Actually, I went to school here."

"Oh," the girl replied, obviously less than impressed. Callie couldn't really blame her, but she felt deflated.

By the time the second bell rang to start class, most of the students were in their desks, but a few were still milling around, talking to each other.

"Take your seats," Callie said, remembering hearing her own teachers say that about a million times. What else had they said? The kids settled and she stared out over approximately thirty expressionless faces. Everyone was waiting for her to do something. Oh, boy.

"Mr. Lightfoot left some work," she said with authority.

"Word searches?" one of them asked.

"You got it," Callie replied.

"Who are you, anyway?" a tall girl near the front said.

"I'm…uh…Ms. McCarran." She'd forgotten to write her name on the board and she wasn't going to do it now. She knew better than to turn her back on them.

"You'd better take attendance." The only boy in the room shorter than she was pointed to the pad Dane had showed her.

"Right." Attendance. Callie began, sometimes having to repeat names two and three times before she heard the response. She was beginning to think they were doing it on purpose. *Quiet confidence.* She handed the word searches to the short boy and asked him to give them out. He'd barely gotten started when the classroom door burst open and a big kid in baggy pants and a black T-shirt strode in. He dropped his books on the desk with a loud bang and then jammed himself into the seat, his legs sprawling in front of him. He was a good five minutes late.

"Excuse me," Callie said sharply, before she noticed a couple of kids in the front row shaking their heads.

"That's Junior," one of them whispered, as if it explained everything.

"Oooh-kay," Callie said softly. Junior sat and stared into the distance while the rest of the students either got out pencils and started the word search or took a cue from their gigantic classmate and stared into space.

With the exception of Junior's grand entrance, the period passed without incident and Junior left more quietly than he had arrived, but Callie remained on edge, waiting for…she didn't know what. But whatever it was, she wanted to be ready.

The rest of the classes proved livelier, with chattier kids, possibly because they were finally waking up, and more personal questions, which she deflected with dry replies before she managed by some miracle and a lot of bluffing to get the students working or quiet. She had a few behavioral problems, but faced them down; a few boys who tried to hit on her, which she ignored. One helpful girl told her she didn't need to be so jumpy. Callie hadn't realized it showed, and made an effort to tone down her jumpiness.

Tyler Michaels, the guy who'd leered at Denise Logan in the café during Callie's interview, was in one of her classes. Other than acting like an overly confident rich-kid-chick-magnet, he hadn't been any kind of problem. But seeing him reminded her that Denise worked at the school in some tucked away office. Callie would have said hello earlier if she'd remembered, but she'd been thinking of little except surviving the day when she'd first arrived at the school.

When the teacher dismissal bell rang at three-thirty, Callie returned her keys to the office.

"Did you have a good day?" Mrs. Serrano asked politely.

"Pretty good," Callie replied. Would she rather be a temp in an office? A seasonal store worker? A gofer/number cruncher during tax season? A backup butcher in a slaughterhouse? You bet. Unfortunately, those jobs were not available. So subbing it was. At least for now.

"Is Denise Logan here today?"

"She was," Mrs. Serrano replied. "Her day ends at two o'clock."

"Oh, that's right."

"Can I give her a message?"

"No," Callie said. "I'll see her next time I'm here."

The Neon barely made it across town. And Wesley was not a very big town. She would have been sunk had she been in San Francisco or Denver. Callie had to get the car in to R&M Auto soon. Her two-hundred-dollar lease was turning out to be a bad investment.

When she got home, she took off her school clothes and tossed them in a heap in the closet. The school had no air-conditioning and the denim skirt and yellow cotton camp shirt were gross. She slipped into her tech pants, a cami and sandals, then went out the back door to get her bike. It wasn't exactly where she'd left it. Either gremlins or Hobarts had been here. Shaking her head, she wheeled the contraption out the back gate into the alley and started the ten-block walk to Nathan's house.

She'd walked only a few blocks when a car came up behind her, traveling slowly. Callie automatically moved up onto the sidewalk, but the engine continued to purr behind her. She cast a glance over her shoulder and saw a teenager driving one hell of a sports car.

"Hey," the kid called out the passenger window. "Didn't I see you at the school today?"

"Maybe," Callie said without slowing. The car edged closer to the side of the street, still shadowing her.

"It's hot." He said the word *hot* in a way that set Callie's teeth on edge. "I can give you a...*ride* to wherever you're going."

Oh, yeah. This kid thought he was a smooth one. "No, thanks."

"You sure?"

"I'm sure." Callie looked over at him again and suddenly recognized the kid—or rather she recognized him as being related to the boy who had annoyed Denise during their interview. This had to be Tyler Michaels's older brother, Mitch. Well, he wasn't going to harass her—even if he was Vince Michaels's kid.

"Positive," Callie called, putting her head down and walking as fast as she could with the disabled bike. The car continued to follow her.

"It must be hard pushing that bike. How about I push the bike and you drive the car?"

"How about you drive away and leave me alone?" Callie replied sharply.

To her surprise, Mitch Michaels laughed appreciatively.

"Have it your way. I'll see you around."

"Not if I see you first," Callie muttered as the blue sports car cruised down the street and around the corner.

NATHAN WAS IN THE GARAGE, cleaning the grease off a gear. The radio was on, playing oldies, and he hadn't heard her walk up the cement driveway in her rubber-soled sandals. She stood for a moment, watching him work, a frown of concentration pulling his dark eyebrows together. In spite of the heat, he was wearing long pants. She recalled the days when all he wore were cutoff jeans, slung low on his hips. He'd thought he was such a twig, but Callie had appreciated the long lean muscles that came from hundreds of miles put on his bike. And though he was still lean, he was anything but a twig. The muscles in his forearms flexed as he worked, making her even more aware of just how attractive he'd become.

And then he looked up, his blue eyes connecting with hers and for one brief second she felt as if she was eighteen again and in love with Nathan Marcenek. But his expression clouded and the moment was lost.

Callie wanted it back. She felt an odd welling of sadness and regret, very much like she'd been feeling as she mourned for Grace. She started pushing the flat-tired bike into the garage, her own muscles flexing with the effort. Somewhere in that tall, muscular body was her old friend Nate Marcenek. Yeah, she'd screwed him over, but she wanted to make amends. She wanted her friend back.

CALLIE MANHANDLED THE BIKE with its two flat tires into the garage, a V of sweat between her breasts and damp, dark blond tendrils curling around her face. She brushed the hair away from her forehead with her wrist.

"You pushed it all the way from your house?"

"I needed the exercise."

He didn't think so. She was fit and firm. Every part of her.

"Thanks for doing this," she said, with a tentative half smile. She must have noticed his lack of response, though, because after a few seconds the smile faded.

He felt crummy, treating her like this, but he needed to stay in control. He needed to stop feeling this pull toward her, as if she was the Callie he'd fallen in love with. He studied her old bike. And it was indeed Callie's old bike. The Trek 920. He probably still had parts for it in his heap of extra bike paraphernalia.

"It's been in the shed for over a decade," she said.

"A rough decade from the looks of it."

"The shed isn't totally weatherproof," she agreed. "Dust in the summer, moisture in the winter."

He put a hand on the tattered bar extenders and Callie let go as he examined the patient.

"I'm going to have to order some parts."

"All right. Just tell me how much it costs."

"You can count on it." Twelve years ago he wouldn't have dreamed of charging Callie. But that was twelve years ago and so much had changed.

Callie wandered over to the wall where he had his

bikes hanging—two mountain bikes and a road bike. "These are nice. You've come up in the world, Nate."

"One of the perks of being steadily employed."

"I wouldn't know about that."

He looked up from the gears, which were impacted with dried grease and dirt. "Have you ever been steadily employed?"

She shrugged. "Not that I recall."

"So just freelancing and temp jobs."

"I haven't gone hungry yet."

"Amazing."

"I like to be able to move on when I need to." The comment hung in the air and for a moment they stared at each other, Callie silently daring him to go ahead and say something snide about her moving on, and Nate wondering if he should.

"Must be nice," he said instead, taking the high road, since lately he'd been spending too much time on the low.

"No complaints," Callie replied hollowly. She fixed her gaze on the bikes, but he didn't think she was seeing them.

Oh, well. He went back to the gears. He'd have to take the assembly apart and clean one component at a time.

"Speaking of temporary jobs, I substitute taught today," she said conversationally.

"No kidding?" He'd had no idea she'd been considering something like that. "What class did you sub for?"

"Sophomore English." She gave the front tire of the

road bike a lazy spin, then turned back to him. "I'd say of all the jobs I've had, subbing is one of my least favorites. I've never had to watch my back like this before. Kids are scary."

"What else *have* you done?" Nate asked, reaching for the tool kit, remembering how she'd evaded this question the last time he'd asked.

"A little of everything."

She was good at evasion. "Do you need the bike soon?" Nathan asked. "I'm going to have to order a new derailleur."

"Whenever you have time."

He got to his feet—pretty smoothly, he thought, considering the trouble he sometimes had when his damaged muscles seized up. He crossed to his big tool kit.

"What'd you do to your leg?" Callie asked from behind him.

Nathan hoped his spine didn't stiffen visibly. "What do you mean?" he asked casually, opening the lid and plunging a hand inside.

"You were moving stiffly when I saw you at the fire, and you're still stiff."

"Just a muscle problem."

"You know, I found a product that really helps…." When he turned, her voice trailed off, telling him that he was failing in his bid to appear casual and unconcerned. "But I guess you have your own ways to treat muscle injuries."

"Yeah. I've had some experience. Look, Cal," he said, tapping the wrench lightly in his palm. "I'm probably going to have to put your bike aside for tonight. I have some work to edit and I won't be able to do much until I get the parts." *And I want you out of here in case you can still read me as well as I can read you.* He didn't want her asking about his leg. He didn't want to deal with her finding out.

"Well, then, I guess I'll be going."

"Guess so."

Callie smiled with false brightness, then started walking down the driveway. Nathan watched her go, thinking that once upon a time he might have offered her a ride.

CHAPTER SEVEN

NATHAN'S PHONE RANG at midnight, waking him up from a sound sleep. He answered without checking the number.

"Well, you missed out." Suzanne sounded ticked.

"I kind of thought I might have," he agreed, rolling over on his back in bed and dropping an arm over his eyes.

"Because you didn't send in an application packet?"

"Yeah. That's pretty much why."

Suzanne sighed. "Aren't you even tempted to get back into the game?"

Nathan's mouth twitched. "I'm in the game."

"You're in the minors. Will you at least come up to the city to visit for a few days sometime?"

"Like when the paper doesn't need to be edited?"

"Like when you take a vacation." There was a pause before she said suspiciously, "You've been there over a year. You do take a vacation, don't you?"

Nathan let his silence answer. "Damn it, Nathan. You *are* nuts."

"Let me know if something else opens up."

"When haven't I?" Suzanne asked with a sniff. "For all the good it does. A lot of wasted time and effort—"

"So how are *you* doing?" Nathan cut into her rant before she warmed up.

"Fair to middling," Suzanne responded in a normal tone. "I take a vacation every now and then, you see…." And the rant was on again.

Nathan hung up a few minutes later, smiling in spite of himself and having promised to consider the vacation idea.

Truth be told, he wouldn't mind getting away. He was busy here in Wesley, and near family, but…he was restless. His dad would tell him he was a damned fool for questioning a near-perfect situation, but Nathan couldn't shake the feeling that maybe he wanted more than the same old stressful thing, day in and day out.

At one time he'd wanted a more adventurous life, less certainty in his days—right up until the world had exploded around him. Did he still want that?

What would he have done if the Wesley job hadn't opened up while he was recuperating?

CALLIE SPENT THE NEXT two days at the high school, substituting for shop class. She'd almost backed out when she'd discovered the subject, but Mrs. Serrano informed her that shop became a study hall when the instructor was absent. Apparently the teacher, Mr. Carstensen, who'd been there when Callie had attended school, didn't want the uninitiated supervising kids armed with power tools. Callie appreciated his far-sighted approach to substitute teacher safety.

The Neon had made the trip to the high school grudgingly both days, but thankfully, Callie managed to snag a cancellation slot at R&M Auto. She just hoped the car lasted the two more days until the appointment so she didn't have to hire a tow truck.

Shop class was easier to manage than the other classes she'd subbed for at the high school—perhaps because of the teacher fear factor. Fear of Mr. C., not herself. She spent the time watching kids pretend to study—although a few actually did appear to be focusing on the words in front of them—and outlining some ideas for her next interview. The doll maker. He was a guy who'd learned to sew in the military, during the Vietnam War, though she didn't know in what capacity. Now, with the help of the Internet, he was making a living selling the folk dolls he'd once made as a hobby.

Her article about Denise had appeared in last week's paper, and Callie had yet to catch up with her to find out if she'd been satisfied. Callie had hoped to see her the last day she subbed for shop class, but Denise had been gone by the time she'd dropped the keys off.

Dane had been in the office, though, and walked Callie to her car, where he asked if she wanted to stop at the café for a malted. She'd laughed, but turned him down.

"I'll have you know," he said with a glint of humor in his blue eyes, "I don't give up easily. I'm a competitor."

"I'll keep that in mind," Callie said drily as she yanked the Neon's door open.

"See you next time you're here, which will probably be when? Tomorrow?" Dane propped a foot against her tire.

"As a matter of fact, yes."

"Then I guess," he said with a charming smile, as he stepped away from the car, "I'll see you soon."

Callie pulled out of the lot a few seconds later, not exactly certain how she felt about the Great Dane. But it was nice to have a guy treat her well for a change. Too bad it wasn't the right guy.

"Whose piece of crap bike is this?" Seth edged around the bike as if he might catch a disease from it.

"Callie's," Nathan said from where he was working on his own bike.

Seth squinted at him from across the garage. "Why do you have Callie's bike? You two hooking up again?"

"Hardly."

"Hey, no one would blame you for taking a shot," Seth said, frowning as he ran a finger over the tattered rubber on the bar extenders. "I mean, yeah, she burned you, but you know the score now, so you can—" he shrugged "—score."

"Maybe I don't want to score."

"Then I feel very, very bad for you."

Nathan opened the door to the kitchen and Seth followed him inside, going straight to the fridge for a beer. He was there to discuss their father's last doctor's visit, as soon as Garrett arrived.

Seth popped the top and drank deeply before wiping the foam off his mouth with the back of his hand. He looked as if he wanted to give advice on scoring, but fortunately, Garrett showed up then, tapping on the side door before coming into the kitchen. Being the older, more mature brother, he actually nodded at the fridge and asked, "May I?" before opening it.

"Help yourself," Nathan said as his brother emerged with two bottles, one of which he pressed into Nate's hands.

Fortified by Stella Artois, the brothers settled at the kitchen table for the John Marcenek powwow.

"I'll be surprised if he goes back to the doctor willingly," Seth said. "I had a bitch of a time getting him there, because he hadn't been taking his medication and he was shifty about it." He took a pull from the bottle. "I'm glad my turn's over."

Nathan muttered a curse. "Maybe we'll have to start double teaming."

"Maybe," Seth agreed. "Anyway, he's not been taking his meds because they make him tired. And the one he really needs leads to constipation. The old man isn't putting up with that shit—no pun intended—so he quit taking them. His blood pressure is through the roof. I think the doc shamed him into going back on the meds, but short of handing him the pills and doing a finger sweep after he takes them, I don't know what we can do."

"Well, that is good news," Garrett said, setting his beer aside. "Where's the Scotch?" He pushed his chair back.

"Don't you have shift tonight?" Nathan asked as Garrett opened the cupboard above the fridge.

"I traded." He pulled out the Laphroaig.

"No," Nathan said. "That's for me. Go for the cheap stuff."

Garrett reluctantly put the bottle back and pulled out the Speyburn.

"Better," Nathan said, turning back to Seth, who was watching Garrett.

"You're the one who went for the free rent," Seth said. "With privilege comes responsibility."

"Bite me." Garrett set the bottle down along with three shot glasses. He'd jumped at the chance to live in the house next door that had been a rental unit while the brothers were growing up. John had rented the house cheap to anyone who passed muster—and agreed to watch the boys while he was on night shift. After Seth had graduated high school, John had stopped renting the second house, tired of the repair work that was part of being a landlord, and when Garrett had come back to town after police academy, he'd happily moved into it.

Now he wasn't so happy.

"I can't handle Dad single-handedly."

"We're not asking you to do that. We're asking you to see that he takes his meds every day."

"Fine." He looked up at Nathan. "Whose crappy bike is that in the garage?"

"Callie's."

"You aren't—"

"None of your freaking business. All right?"

"He's not," Seth said, as he turned his shot glass upside down. Like their father, he was a beer man through and through.

Nathan muttered a curse. "Okay, here's the deal. Garrett, you make sure he's still on his meds. I'm going to drop by and explain that if he doesn't do as the doctor asks, then there's no way he's passing next year's physical and he's off the fire crew."

No one argued with him. Nathan was always the guy who handled the rough stuff with his dad, because he was the one who was used to being yelled at.

"What does Seth do?" Garrett asked after taking a slow sip from the shot glass.

"Seth stops by daily to cheer him up."

"Cool." Seth lifted his beer.

"And to make him lose thirty pounds."

Seth sneered. "Oh, yeah. I can do that."

"Make him walk with you. Maybe we can buy him a bike."

"With a jumbo reinforced frame," Seth said morosely.
"Whatever it takes."

CALLIE RECEIVED HER FIRST substitute request from the
elementary school, and discovered that sixth graders
weren't as intimidating as sophomores, but they were
more exhausting. In an odd way, though, they seemed
more mature than the sophomores. Maybe it was because they were still kids for the most part, acting their
age instead of trying to act like they were Callie's peers.

The sixth-grade teacher, Mr. Jones, had left copious
notes. Callie knew what time to start a lesson, what time
to finish it. And if she hadn't had notes, she would have
had Sienna, the Helper Girl. Helper Girl was fine in the
beginning, but by the end of the day she was beginning
to grate on Callie's last nerve. Callie sucked it up,
though. She had a feeling that any kid who acted like
this had issues elsewhere in her life. Who was Callie to
add to them?

After school she had dismissal duty, which involved
standing on the play field and encouraging the kids to
go home. Sienna was there by her side.

"What grades are the Hobart kids in?" Callie asked,
spotting her little neighbors playing on the swing.

"Lucas is in fourth and Lily is in fifth. They're
weird," Sienna added conversationally.

*Do you mean weird like hanging with a teacher after
school instead of going home?*

"We're all a little strange," Callie said drily, making Sienna laugh.

"You're not. You're nice."

Not according to the people at Grace's memorial service.

"Oh," Sienna said excitedly. "There's my mom!" A shiny pickup pulled up behind the school. "Bye, Miss McCarran! I hope you come back!"

"Bye, Sienna. Thanks for the help today."

The girl spun around to wave, then ran to the truck. The woman driving looked sane and happy to see her daughter. Okay, maybe it was hard to tell who had issues and who didn't. Maybe Sienna had been born helpful and needy.

The Hobart kids had disappeared while Callie was waving to Sienna, and the rest of the students were beginning to drift off the playground, meeting parents or walking home. Callie glanced at her watch. Five more minutes to freedom.

A long five minutes. It was blazing hot standing out on the play field, but eventually Callie got into the oven that went by the name of Neon, and the little car coughed its way to the repair shop. She had a brief consultation with the mechanic, who promised to call as soon as he had a diagnosis, then she declined his offer of a ride and walked home. Quite possibly one or two of her sub checks would be going toward the repair of a car she didn't even own. That was foolish, but she would be even more of a fool to head out across the

Nevada desert in a car that sounded like the Neon. When she left town, that was.

The house seemed quiet after spending the day with twenty-four sixth graders. Callie shucked off her school clothes and put on a tank top and khaki shorts. She dropped ice cubes into a glass, filled it with water and headed out to the shade in the backyard rather than turning on the noisy old air-conditioning unit.

She could hear the Hobart kids playing in the lot on the other side of the cedar fence. They didn't have many toys scattered in their yard, but they did seem to get a lot of mileage out of the baseball.

Callie had yet to see an adult on the premises other than the very blonde woman she assumed was the mother, although she had to admit that was probably because she only had a view of the side of the house unless she was out on the street. The front lawn and porch were obscured by thick honeysuckle bushes, and the carport was on the opposite side.

Funny, though, that she saw the kids a lot and the adults hardly ever. And it still bothered her, especially after she'd once again seen the boy out after dark and the house completely dark. Again she'd knocked and again got no answer.

AFTER FED EX DELIVERED the bike parts to Nate's office, he took an early out and went home to fix Callie's bike. He'd worked until ten the previous evening and took files home with him today, so it wasn't as if Vince Michaels wasn't getting his money's worth and the paper wouldn't come out on time.

It was peaceful tinkering in his garage, with no phones or machines in the background. Plus he was looking forward to getting the bike back to Callie and being done with the obligation.

He loaded it in the back of his small truck and drove over to Callie's a little after four o'clock. She was walking down the sidewalk from the direction of town when he pulled onto her street. They arrived at Grace's house at the same time.

"Where's your car?" he asked as he hefted the bike out of the truck and set it down. It bounced on its tires.

"Still in the shop. You weren't the only one who had to order parts. The bike looks like new."

"You subbed today." She was wearing makeup and her hair was down.

"Yeah."

"You should have told me," he said, holding the bike by the seat.

"Oh? Why?" she asked innocently. "Would you have given me a ride?"

"Maybe."

"Well, walking isn't that big a deal to me. I just left a half hour early."

"When's the car done?"

"Tomorrow."

"Are you subbing tomorrow?"

"No."

"All right."

"Careful, Nate." He looked up at her. "You sound like you might care."

He just shook head.

"Did you write me up a bill?"

"Not yet."

"Well, until you get round to it, how about dinner or something?" She smiled that old Callie smile, which in turn made him want to smile back.

"I don't think so."

Her face fell. "I won't walk out on you."

"I have work to do, and if you're going to have that next article in on time, so do you."

"It's done. I e-mailed it. Didn't you get it?"

"Uh, no." He didn't want her to know he'd taken off a couple hours early, planning to make up the time tonight, in order to fix the bike once the parts came in. "I've been busy."

She studied his face for a moment, as if trying to figure out what he was thinking. Her eyes shifted to the house behind him as a car with a worn muffler pulled up in front.

"Are you familiar with the Hobart family?" she asked. Nathan glanced over his shoulder to see a tall man in a cowboy shirt and jeans get out of the car.

"They're from up north," he said, turning back to her. "They have a bit of a rep."

"A Hobart family lives in the house across the lot there. The kids come into my backyard sometimes."

"Casing the joint?"

"I hope not. They're nine and eight."

Nathan nodded politely, wondering why he was getting a neighborhood update.

"I don't think their parents take very good care of them."

"Why's that?"

"Because I see them out at night a lot. And the house is dark. I've been wondering if anyone is even home at night with them."

"You've been watching them that closely?"

"I noticed the little boy at the fire where I saw you and Garrett. His sister was dragging him home from it, so yeah, I've noticed."

"Did you talk to the parents?"

"No one answered the door that night."

"You're sure the kids were in there?"

"Yeah."

"But you have no way of knowing whether or not there was an adult."

"Alice said there's a grandma, but I've never seen her."

"That doesn't mean she doesn't exist."

Callie was still staring at the house, a tiny frown drawing her eyebrows together. "I guess."

"Callie?" She glanced back at him, her eyes distant. He recalled some of her crusades in junior high and high school. Once she bit into a cause, she refused to let go. "The Hobarts are not people to mess with."

"Damn, Nate. Are you saying I should ignore what's going on?"

"No. I'll be the first in line to turn someone in for child abuse. I'm saying be sure of your facts. Are the kids overly skinny? Do they have marks on them? Wear raggedy clothes?"

"There are other forms of abuse. Like, say, neglect."

The man who'd gone in the house came out again, with the two kids bounding around him, healthy and energetic. Nathan turned a serious gaze back on Callie, wondering what she saw.

"On a one-to-ten scale, how sure are you that the kids are being neglected? By sure, I mean hard evidence."

Callie pressed her lips together momentarily. "Four," she said grudgingly. "Going by hard evidence."

"Be careful here, Cal."

"Thanks for tuning up the bike for me. I'm looking forward to riding." It was pretty obvious that she wouldn't have minded having someone to ride with. Nate didn't make the offer, because part of him really wanted to and he didn't totally trust that part of himself.

When Callie was like this, when he was able to push past issues aside, then he could see being friends again—or rather, he could if they hadn't once moved beyond friendship. He still felt the sexual attraction to her. Strongly. Had she just come back right after dumping him, yeah, maybe he would have swallowed his pride and tossed his hat back in the ring. Enjoyed the moment. But now when he thought of being her lover, trust issues reared their ugly heads. Logically, he could tell himself that his leg didn't matter. But honestly? It mattered to him. His head was messed up about it. He was ashamed of something out of his control, and he couldn't help feeling that way.

Callie seemed distant as he left, quite possibly because he'd done his best to make her that way. He didn't want to go to dinner with her and he didn't buy her theory that the kids next door were neglected. He'd seen them playing in the lot and they looked like healthy, happy kids.

He had to admit, though, that it bothered him to see Callie distressed, since it didn't fit with his idea of a selfish Callie. Selfish Callie made it easy to stand back, keep his distance. He didn't particularly want that to change.

When he got home, just in case she was onto something, Nathan called Garrett and asked him what he knew about the Hobart family. His answer was exactly what Nathan had expected. They kept to themselves, and if no one bothered them, they didn't bother anybody.

"Callie's concerned about the kids." Nathan opened a cupboard. He hadn't shopped lately and didn't have much selection. Instant macaroni and cheese, or soup.

"How so?"

"She says they spend a lot of time unsupervised." He pulled out a can of soup, then put it back. He didn't want to go out and eat alone. Maybe he should have gone to dinner with Callie.

"So did we."

"She seems to think these parents are leaving them alone while they work at night."

"Evidence?"

"That's the sticking point. I think it's all just gut feeling, but if these kids are being left to their own devices…" Nathan pulled a Chinese dinner out of the freezer and popped it in the microwave.

"Remember when she talked you into trying to set the pound dogs free when you were eleven?"

"These are kids, Garrett."

"I'll ask around unofficially, see if anyone's heard anything. I'll check with the school, too. Talk to their teacher."

"Thanks."

"So…spending much time with Callie?"

"I fixed her bike."

"Don't get suckered in again, Nathan."

"Your faith in my common sense is overwhelming." He punched the microwave buttons with unnecessary force.

"I know the power of the double X chromosome."

"Shove it."

CHAPTER EIGHT

WHEN CALLIE GOT HER CALL from Mrs. Serrano, asking her to sub for Dane Gerard while he was away for a basketball game, she made it a point to get to the school early enough to stop by Denise's office and say hello.

"I loved the article," Denise said the moment she saw Callie standing in the doorway of her tiny office. "You did such a good job of getting across the difficulties of my situation without making anyone look bad or me look like a whiner. Very matter-of-fact. I loved it."

"Great," Callie said. Heaven knew she'd written a few articles in her time that weren't so appreciated. And Denise's warmth and sincerity were a nice change from the reception she'd received from many people in town. Although she had to admit that people seemed to be forgetting about her now. She'd bumped into one of Grace's club friends and actually got a cool hello.

"By the way, who are you today?"

"Mr. Gerard. Algebra and calculus. I sure hope he left some word search puzzles...."

Denise laughed. "I doubt you'll have to teach calculus. So you're doing all right with the subbing?"

"Right now I have the utmost respect for people who do this for a living." Callie adjusted her leather backpack on her shoulder. "I'd better be going so I can gear up for the day. I just wanted to say hi."

She'd started toward the door when a thought struck her and she turned back. Denise cocked her head curiously. "Do you notice much about the gawkers when you fight fires?"

"Sometimes."

"Have you ever noticed some young, very blond kids there? Around eight or nine years old?"

"You know, I have. I figured their parents must be serious fire groupies to bring the entire family, but I don't know who they are."

Callie felt a surge of anger. "Thanks."

"Hey," Denise called after Callie had left the office. She reversed course and stuck her head in the door. "Would you like to come out with the staff to The Supper Club Friday after school for decompression?"

"Isn't that for real teachers?"

"It's for anyone who survives a day with kids."

Callie laughed. "I'll probably try to make it."

"No probably. Plan on it. The more teachers get to know you, the more jobs you'll get."

After that day, however, Callie wasn't sure how many more jobs she wanted to get at the high school.

Algebra went fine. The sophomores and freshmen were familiar with her, and she'd identified the players.

Calculus, on the other hand, was her first ever upperclassman group. For the most part it was quieter, the kids more on task as they worked on problems Dane had left. But Mitch Michaels was in the class, and he obviously recalled her as the woman with the bike who he'd tried to pick up. He kept making eye contact and smiling in a not-so-innocent way.

At first Callie ignored him, thinking maybe he'd get the hint, but by the end of class she'd had enough. When the bell rang, dismissing school, Mitch left with the rest of the kids, but five minutes later he came sauntering back in.

"Hello, Mitch," Callie said pleasantly, even though she was speaking through her teeth.

"Miss McCarran." He perched his butt on one of the desks, an indication he was in no hurry to leave.

"Do you need something?" She cringed inwardly as the words left her mouth, and for a moment she thought he was going to tell her exactly what he needed. The kid exuded confidence, but it was an unsettling kind of confidence. The kind with sexual overtones that stood the hairs up on the back of her neck.

"No. I just thought I'd drop by and talk. I know subs don't have a lot to do between three and three-thirty."

"Oh, I'm fine all by myself."

Mitch shifted his gaze to the floor for a moment, a slight smile playing on his lips. Then he looked up with a suggestively arched eyebrow. "I'm graduating at semester."

"Then what?"

"School in California. Cal Poly."

"What are you majoring in?" *And what do I have to do to make you go away?* She was getting an uncomfortable vibe.

His leg swung back and forth casually. Callie recognized the brand on his shoe. A pair of those would set her back a couple sub checks. "Premed probably."

"How nice." Callie folded her hands in front of her and stared at him.

"I guess what I'm getting at is that I am eighteen. Legal."

Callie raised her brows in mock confusion and waited. He shifted slightly, but it wasn't out of discomfort. The boy was too comfortable.

"I know your father," Callie finally said. "We played golf together." Kind of. But she was sticking with the half-truth, because what kind of kid hit on someone who'd played golf with his dad?

This kind of kid. One corner of his handsome mouth curved up. "I play golf, too."

"You'd better leave, Mitch."

He didn't argue. Instead, he acted as if that was part of the game. Maybe it would be part of the game if they were living in a 1960s Sandra Dee movie. They weren't, so Callie continued to apply her stony stare until he left the room. When the door clicked shut behind him, she exhaled. No wonder Denise had been so creeped out by Mitch's younger brother, if she'd already had to put up with this.

Callie finished her note and dropped the keys off at the office, glad the day was over and she was done with students. But she wasn't. Mitch was sitting in his shiny blue sports car, parked a few spaces away from the Neon. The driver's side window was open and he smiled at her when she walked past.

If he followed her out of the lot, she was driving straight to the sheriff's office…but he didn't. Callie watched her mirror the entire way home.

Okay, he hadn't done anything except sit in his car, but he'd sure gotten the message across. He wanted to play.

Fat chance.

When Callie pulled onto her street, glad to be far away from Mitch Michaels, the first thing she noticed was the car parked under the carport of the Hobart house. It would have been hard not to notice it, since it was a hot pink Mustang. The paint was chipped, the bumper dented, but at one time it had probably been a sweet ride.

Later that night there were lights on in the Hobart house. It wasn't exactly lit up like a Christmas tree, but the ground floor had lights on in two rooms. That was promising.

She hoped.

SETH BOUNCED HIS helmet off his thigh as he waited for Nathan to finish the last-minute adjustments to his bike. Nate's Saturday morning ride with his younger brother inevitably became a race, and he needed every advantage.

His injured leg had recovered more than the doctors had hoped, but the nerve and muscle damage were extensive enough that his left leg still had to do more work when he rode. As a result, Seth almost always beat him when they raced around the loop by the river, and being a total brotherly jerk, he also crowed about it. That more than anything endeared his younger brother to Nathan. No sympathy from the kid. Nathan was as uncomfortable with sympathy as he was with his injury.

"Come on," Seth said. "I have a shift later and I want to eat before I go."

Nate popped the wrench back into his tool kit and put the bike back on its wheels. Together they walked to the road and mounted, clicking their shoes into place.

"I have to go back to the office myself."

"You work too many hours."

"Look who's talking. One paying job and two volunteer."

"Yes, but I use my jobs to meet women. Can you say the same?"

No, he couldn't.

"You know," Seth mused, "since you're falling down on the job, maybe I'll find you a woman."

"Yeah, why don't you do that," Nathan said as he put

his head down and started to seriously pedal, leaving his brother behind.

"Blonde, brunette or redhead?" Seth called as he caught up and then sailed past.

"Surprise me!" Nathan yelled after him. He heard Seth give a bark of laughter and began to think that perhaps he'd just made a major error. "No blind dates!" he shouted into the wind.

"Too late," Seth called back. "I'm setting something up and if you back out, you'll hurt her feelings."

"Don't…"

Seth slowed until the two bikes were side by side. "Trust me, Nate. It's for your own good. Time for you to get back on the horse."

"No." It had taken almost a year for Nathan to finally accept the twisted and scarred flesh on his leg as part of him, but he still wasn't wild to share. His leg was ugly, and that was a generous assessment, but it worked and Nathan was alive. For that he'd be ever grateful. But he wasn't ready to put himself out there for anyone.

Head down, Seth started pedaling, acting as if he didn't hear him. Nathan poured everything he had into the pedals and finally pulled ahead of the kid as they reached the city limits. They both slowed, Nate sitting up and drinking from his water bottle, squeezing the rest over the back of his neck and chest.

He didn't mention blind dates as he and Seth rode side by side down the nearly deserted street leading to his house. He wasn't going on a blind date; he'd made that clear. And he didn't want to draw any more lines in the sand, because Seth was a guy who dearly loved to cross lines.

CALLIE DIDN'T KNOW WHAT to make of the situation with the kids next door. During the four days the pink Mustang had been there, the lights and TV went on and off during the appropriate hours. But this morning the car was gone and the house was once again dark in the evening. But the kids were there, playing outside until the sun went down.

Was that nine-year-old girl babysitting her brother all night while the mother worked an evening shift at the casino?

So what should Callie do? When did none-of-her-business shift into her moral duty? She was seriously considering calling Child Protective Services, but maybe there were circumstances she wasn't aware of. Maybe the kids went to a neighbor's house evenings. That would explain the dark house and also let Callie believe these children were being cared for. She needed to believe that.

Callie hadn't been able to find someone to mow her lawn, so in a fit of desperation, she dragged Lawn-Boy out and fought a few rounds with him, losing on a TKO when she pulled the starter cord for the umpteenth time and the handle broke into two pieces, sending her flying back onto her butt with a piece of plastic clutched in her hand. The other part of the handle was still attached to the rope, preventing it from disappearing inside the engine, and Callie decided to admit defeat before she ended up paying to fix something else.

But if she was going to sell this house, she had to mow the lawn. Alice was no help, with her xeriscape gravel, rock and succulent landscaping. Callie was going to have to suck it up and go ask the neighbors for recommendations. What happened to kids who put flyers up at the grocery store? Were they all home playing video games and surfing the Web?

And then to add to the joy that was her life, Mitch Michaels had actually called her landline and asked her on a date that morning, pointing out that when she wasn't working, it wouldn't be a conflict of interest. After turning him down flat and suggesting he never call again, she wondered whether he'd asked her on a dare from a friend, to make fun of her, or whether he really wanted a date.

Didn't matter. If he kept bugging her, she was going to call either his dad or the cops. He was eighteen…maybe Garrett could scare some sense into him. Yeah, Garrett, who liked her so much.

Or maybe Mitch had actually gotten the message and was just saving face.

And maybe it was time to leave, to head back to San Francisco. She could drop the Neon off on the way, before it cost her more money. There'd be no Mitch

Michaels, no worries about the kids next door, no battles with Lawn-Boy.

No more unsettling attraction to Nathan, who wanted nothing to do with her.

Tempting. Callie leaned her palms on the edge of the sink and looked out the window at the overgrown lawn. Very tempting. But she wasn't going to let a bunch of grass, a cranky hunk of machinery, a horny kid and her ex-boyfriend drive her away before she was damned ready to go.

She raised her gaze to the Hobart house across the lot. Nope. She was staying a while longer.

NATHAN RUBBED HIS FINGERS over his eyes, pushing his reading glasses up on top of his head before tossing them carelessly onto the desk.

It was late. He needed to get home. He'd forgone his evening bike ride to finish up at the office, and now his stomach was growling and he was getting a head-ache, though he couldn't tell if it was work related or Callie related.

Seth called as Nathan was leaving the building. "I have your blind date set up."

Nate shut the phone and shoved it in his pocket. It wasn't going to do him much good in the long run, but perhaps he could get his hands on some aspirin or Scotch before Seth found him in person.

No such luck. Seth was parked in front of his house when he got there.

"Turning the phone off isn't going to help. There's nowhere you can hide."

"I don't recall giving the blind date an okay," Nathan said, shouldering his way past his brother to unlock his door.

"You said, 'Surprise me,'" Seth countered with a crooked smile. "Surprise!"

"Who is she?" Nathan dumped his day pack, which he used in place of a briefcase, next to the door.

"New girl at the mine. Her name is Gina."

"Do you know her at all?"

"I've talked to her."

"Then why aren't you dating her?"

"She refuses to take me seriously."

"I wonder why?" Nathan said as he went into the kitchen and opened the fridge. "Could it be the Gumby insignia on your hat?"

Seth shrugged as he accepted a beer. "Honestly, she's not my type, and yeah, Gumby may figure into it. She's more serious than the girls I date."

"Why's she at the mine?"

"She's the new human resources person. And she is good-looking."

Nathan twisted off the beer cap, took a long drink, watching his brother the entire time for some kind of tell.

"Brunette. Smart. *Really* good-looking." Seth glanced away, then back at his brother, all playfulness gone from his expression. "It's time, Nate. You need to get out, even if you don't end up in the sack. You can't use your leg as an excuse forever."

"It took *me* a year to get used to it. How can I expect someone else to…" Hell, he didn't even know how to finish the sentence. "It's not an excuse," he muttered, going to the table to flip through the mail. "But it is damned ugly." And the last Nathan had heard, wild one-night stands were about attraction. The Igor leg would surely throw a damper on that kind of an evening. His wild one-night-stand days were over.

"Wouldn't know. I haven't seen it since it was bandaged up."

"And you're not seeing it tonight."

"Rats." Seth punctuated the word with a quick clench of his fist.

They went into the living room and Seth turned on the TV, watching the Food Network as he finished his beer.

"Man, I love Cat Cora," he said as he tossed the remote over to Nathan and stood. "I need to find a woman who cooks. I'm getting tired of living on Oreos and canned soup."

Nathan had dozed off during the final minutes of the *Iron Chef,* so he had no idea whether or not Cat had dominated. He also didn't care.

Seth stopped at the door. "Here's the deal about the

date. It's a group thing. The mine bought two tables at the Lions Club Crab Feed. You're invited, and Gina will be there."

"Anybody else showing up stag?"

"You're not stag, Nate. You're with Gina. You'll show up?"

"I guess." Maybe his brothers were right. Maybe it was time to get back on the horse. Or to at least spend some time in the pasture getting reacquainted with the animal.

JOHN MARCENEK WAS WORKING on his pickup when Nathan went to see him on Saturday after putting in a half day at work.

"Here to check on me?" John said from beneath the chassis, when he heard the footsteps come into the garage. He rolled out from under the truck on his mechanic's board and sat up, wiping the grease off his hands with the rag he pulled out of his coverall pocket. "Thought you'd be at work. Isn't it Seth's turn to babysit?"

"Are you taking your pills?"

"Yes." He looked shifty, but Nathan had no choice but to believe him.

"Then I'm not here to babysit. I thought you might want to grab a bite."

"Can't. Chester's coming over." John smirked. "That lets you off the hook and now you can go do whatever."

Nathan hooked his thumbs in his belt loops. "I'm not on the hook, Dad."

John stared down at the wood he was sitting on for a long moment. "Look. I appreciate what you guys are doing, but back off, all right? I can take care of myself. I'm only sixty-five, for cripe's sake."

"Yeah."

John got to his feet, his movements awkward because of his bulk. "I heard you're sniffing around Callie McCarran again."

His father had always been a master at changing topics. His favorite technique was to touch a sore spot if he could find one, thus putting his opponent on the defensive.

"Where'd you hear that?" Nathan asked evenly. Because if it was from Seth or Garrett, he was going to have to rearrange their faces.

"Around."

"If it's true, then it's none of your business. And if it's not…same thing, Dad."

"I don't want to see you make an ass out of yourself," John grumbled as he walked over to the workbench and put the ratchet on its place on the Peg-board. "It's one thing to do it when you're eighteen. Another when you're pushing thirty."

Nathan clenched his teeth. He was not going to rise to the bait. It was one thing to get pushed around by your old man at eighteen, another to be pushed around at thirty.

"Besides that," John said, his back to his son as he pumped waterless hand cleaner into his palm, "I don't think she's the kind that'll take the leg well. It'll take a special woman to deal with that."

Nathan just stared at his father's back. What the hell? That was pretty much the last thing he wanted to hear.

"Bye, Dad." He headed for his rig. John said nothing, and Nathan figured his dad had gotten his wish. He was alone. No more babysitter. Had it been Seth who'd stopped by, they would have ended up playing cribbage. Garrett would have dived into the truck engine with him. Nathan got a lecture on why no woman would want him.

He went home, changed into his bike clothes and took off. Why did his dad still bother him so much?

His dad was his dad, and Nathan was going to have to live with the fact that he was not the favorite son. Or the second favorite.

He rode an extra five miles up the soft dirt of the river road, blissfully alone and out of sight of the highway, before he turned around at the party spot where he and his brothers had done things their sheriff father wouldn't have been thrilled about. He came to the fork where the left turn led down to the campsite by the river, and the right one led up a steep hill to the highway. He started up the hill, glancing down at the river as he climbed, then stopped pedaling when he saw the bike lying on its side, abandoned in the middle of the campground.

It looked like Callie's.

He coasted back down the hill. It *was* Callie's bike.

Lying on its side near the stone fire ring. He came to a stop next to it, looked around, his heart beating faster.

He laid his own bike on the ground next to hers, dropped the helmet beside it and headed for the trail leading to the river.

At first he didn't see anything, but then he spotted her in the water, next to the rickety old fishing dock, her head tilted back and eyes closed, her hair floating out behind her.

She was safe and she was beautiful.

Callie had always been beautiful, maybe even more so because she'd always seemed unaware of it. Or perhaps she didn't care. She'd rarely worn makeup when they'd been together, did little more to her hair than pull it into a braid or a ponytail. Now it was shorter, more stylish, but except for the time he'd dropped off the bike, and the first meeting in his office, it had been tied back.

He stood perfectly still on the bank, watching her. Finally he cleared his throat. Startled, Callie spun around in the water. Her expression cleared when she saw it was him.

"What are you doing here?" she asked, standing and wading closer to the shore. As she walked into shallower water, he could see that she was wearing her biking clothes—Lycra shorts and a body-hugging top, which, interestingly, was transparent when wet. He felt ridiculous standing on the shore fully dressed in long athletic pants, too hot for the weather.

"Come on in. The water is wonderful."

"Normal people don't swim in October," he pointed out. The water lapped at her thighs, which were firm and fit from all that walking, biking and trekking she did in the line of duty.

"Thank global warming. It's not usually this hot in October. Why're you here?"

"I saw your bike lying on its side and got concerned."

"It doesn't have a kickstand so I had to lay it down."

"Really?" he asked, as if receiving new and vital information. She hit the heel of her palm on the water, splashing him.

Nathan took a few steps toward the water's edge, leaned down and picked up a flat stone. He tossed it and it skipped six times before sinking.

"You've lost your touch."

"Think you could do better?"

Callie started toward him, water running in rivulets off her body. She stopped in the shallows, considered the pebbles at her feet, then leaned down and picked one up.

He really wished her tank top left a little something to the imagination. Nathan idly dropped his hand and did his best to arrange himself before she looked up.

She smiled at him once she had her stone, and it was hard to tell whether it was in answer to his challenge or because she was aware that she was turning him on. She pulled her arm back, then let the stone go. One, two, three, four, five, six...and a blip.

"I win."

"That last one wasn't a full skip," Nathan said.

"But you didn't have anything past six."

He couldn't argue with that. "Do you have a shirt or something with you?"

"Why?"

"Your breasts are showing through your top."

Callie glanced down abruptly, then looked slowly back at him, checking him out in the process. He hoped by some miracle she missed his hard-on. He knew when her eyes finally hit his face that she hadn't. She smiled.

"Nothing you haven't seen before," she said.

"I thought you might not want anyone else to see them."

"I have a shirt. It's by the dock." She took a step back. "Come into the water, Nate."

Again he shook his head, knowing he was being invited to do more than simply come for a swim.

"You can strip down to your shorts like you used to. I'll never tell."

But she would see a whole lot more of him than he was willing to show.

"I need to get back to town."

"Fine." She took a few steps toward him, slipped and regained her balance without going under. She held out her hand for stability, and the second he reached for it he realized he'd just fallen for the oldest trick on record. The next thing he knew he was off balance and being yanked forward. He landed with a giant splash and then surfaced, spitting water.

Callie laughed. "Man, Nate. You need to sharpen your instincts."

"Maybe I just let you do that," he sputtered.

"I'd like to believe it." She reached to cup his face, smiling up at him as tiny streams of water ran down from her hair. She was going to kiss him. She was going to see just how far she could push this moment.

He put his hands on her wrists before she could press herself against him, held her at a distance.

"I've felt wood before, Nate."

Fine. Let her think he was being modest. Anything was better than her pressing her gorgeous thighs against his wet nylon pants and feeling his hard, twisted wreck of a leg.

Callie took a step back and he released her wrists. "You are going to have one hell of a lonely life, Nate, if you find yourself so unable to forgive. People make mistakes. I made a mistake. I'm damned sorry about it."

"Me, too, Callie." Because if she hadn't made that mistake and hadn't kept making it by refusing to answer his calls and letters, they might have settled down and had a family. Or they might have gone their separate ways, but with closure. And if one of those circumstances had prevailed, he had a feeling he'd be a whole man today—in every way.

As he walked out of the river, his hair and face were

already drying, but the nylon clung to his leg. He hoped the damp fabric didn't show too much, or that Callie was too pissed off to notice—which she might well be, since she stayed in the water.

Or so he figured, because he walked up the trail and around the bend to the campsite without looking back.

CHAPTER NINE

CALLIE SAT ON THE DOCK and dried in the late afternoon sun. It was past time to get to work on her research for the next article, but still she sat, hugging her arms around her knees, trying to contain an aching sense of loss that had come out of nowhere when Nate had walked away.

She was going to have to cry uncle on this one. It was beginning to hurt too much, beating herself on the rock known as Nathan Marcenek.

She'd honestly believed that, given time, Nate would come round to her way of thinking, that they could be friends. Maybe even more…in a friendly ships-that-pass-in-the-night sort of way. Except that Nate wasn't going to let it happen.

Today she'd gotten a glimpse of the old Nate, the one she'd loved. A tiny peek, just enough to make everything she'd ever felt for him burst alive again, and then he was gone, leaving her emptier and more alone than ever.

Damn it, she was used to being alone. She thrived on it.

Or rather, she had. Alone didn't feel so good anymore, and that bothered her. A lot.

She'd made some superficial friends since arriving back in Wesley—Denise Logan, Dane Gerard and some other teachers at the high school. Superficial friends were the only kind she ever had. They demanded nothing of her and she returned the favor.

But she had hoped for something different with Nate. She'd wanted him to be a real friend, as he'd once been, maybe a lover, as he'd almost been. And she'd wanted him to ultimately understand when she had to leave, to recognize that wanderlust was part of her and that she simply couldn't stay put very long. Six months had been her record.

What she wanted was selfish, really, and she was simply going to have to give it up.

Callie rose to her feet, brushed the sand and weathered wood splinters off her Lycra shorts and started climbing the trail to where she'd left her bike. She'd call the real estate agent tomorrow, get the ball rolling on the house. The market was dead at the moment, so a sale could take a while. She'd have a place to live while she finished the articles for Vince Michaels—and they were for him, since Nate wouldn't have bought them if she hadn't gone to his boss first. Nate honestly wanted nothing to do with her and it had taken her this long to get the message, loud and clear.

CALLIE WAS WRITING THAT night, late, when she saw headlights pull into the carport at the Hobarts' place. Lights went on inside the house before the car beams were turned off. Someone had been inside waiting.

Callie went to the window. Her living room was dark, the only light coming from her computer monitor, so she wasn't concerned about being caught spying. Mrs. Hobart got out of the pink Mustang, wearing black pants and a white long-sleeved shirt, the casino dealer's uniform, and climbed the stairs. The boy stepped out into the light, holding the screen door open for his mother, who seemed to be halfheartedly scolding him—maybe for being up so late. It was 1:30 A.M.

Callie went back to her computer, but didn't put her hands on the keyboard. What was the best way to handle this? She didn't want to hurt the family, but it was wrong for these kids to be alone at that age until this early in the morning.

The next afternoon Callie walked over to the Hobarts' and knocked on the door. The car was still at the curb, so the mom must be working the five-to-one evening shift. Callie automatically reached for the doorbell, then remembered from her previous visit that it didn't work. Instead, she knocked on the screen door. A dog started yapping, the noise getting closer as footsteps approached. The blonde woman opened the door, weary and far from welcoming.

"Hi. I'm Callie McCarran. Your neighbor across the lot."

The woman nodded, waiting, the frown still pulling her overly plucked eyebrows together.

"I wanted to introduce myself."

She nodded without offering her name, looking out from around the door as if it was a protective barrier. She wasn't making this easy.

"I substitute teach and I've seen your kids at school and in the neighborhood." This wasn't going well, judging from the woman's expression. "If you ever needed a babysitter or anything, I'd be happy to let them stay at my place while you're working."

"Why're you offering to babysit my kids?"

"I just noticed that sometimes they're home alone, and if they needed a place to stay while you were at work—"

"Have you been spying on my kids? How the hell do you know they're home alone?"

Callie couldn't help drawing back at Mrs. Hobart's aggressive tone. Oh, yeah, this was going great.

"Look," the woman continued, "you stay away from the kids and you keep your nose out of my business, or I'll call the sheriff on you."

And wouldn't Garrett have a field day with that?

"My kids are just fine and I *do* have someone who baby sits them when I work—not that it's any of your business. My mom is here!"

Callie backed away a few steps, but the woman

wasn't done. "The last thing I'd ever do is to let them stay with someone who's been watching them! If I…" Her mouth worked for a moment, but words failed her in her rage. Finally she simply slammed the door shut. Callie could hear her heels on the hardwood floor, followed by muffled shouts of "Lily! Lucas! I want to talk to you!"

Callie walked back to her own house, numb and embarrassed and…damn, she didn't know what she was feeling, but it was bad. And if there was a grandmother in that house, she loved the dark.

The next morning, the dream came as it usually did, when Callie wasn't quite fully awake. There was the sharp burning in her nostrils, the images and sensations that she was on the edge of recognizing before fear took over and blurred everything except her need to escape. Hands. Once again she had the impression of hands.

After the first surge of fright brought her to sit up in bed, Callie took slow, steady breaths through her nose until the sensations faded.

Who had triggered the dream this time? Nate or the neighbor? Both encounters had been unsettling, but Nate had hurt her, while the other had merely put her on the defensive. Her bet was on Nate again.

She pushed the covers back and got out of bed.

She'd hoped to write that day, since there'd been no sub call, but the dream always made her writing suffer.

She could put words on paper, but there was no flair. It was as if she was afraid to let her mind go, in case it stumbled on a dark secret behind the nightmare. If there was a secret, the original trigger, it had happened before her father's disappearance, because she'd had the dream before she came to live with Grace.

Callie had considered hypnosis at one point, but ultimately decided against it. The dream came and went. If she was dealing with an actual memory, though… well…once recalled, she'd have it forever. Nope. She was going with head in the sand. If her mind was protecting her, she was going to let it do its job.

Half an hour later the landline rang. She assumed it was the real estate agent, and hoped it wasn't Mitch Michaels again. He hadn't called after she'd shut him down, but he had hung around her room at school the last time she'd subbed, had tried to walk her to her car. He didn't get the concept of no means no.

She picked up the phone and said hello, ready to put the receiver back down again if it was Mitch. Thankfully, the voice on the other end of the phone was deeper and vaguely familiar.

"Hi, Callie. It's Dane Gerard."

"Oh. Hi, Dane." Relieved, she wondered why the heck he was calling. Mrs. Serrano handled the sub calls.

"So, did you enjoy calculus class?"

Callie laughed. "Oh, yes. Tons of fun."

"The kids said you did a great job watching them suffer through their test."

"I'm an educational sadist. What can I say?"

"I was wondering…the Lions Club crab dinner is coming up in a few days and we have an extra chair at our table. An educational sadist would be a wonderful addition."

"Uh…" Did she want to go out with the Great Dane? A picture of Nate walking away from her at the river popped into her head. "Sure. Sounds good."

"Pick you up at, say, six-thirty?"

"How about I meet you there?"

After the briefest of hesitations, Dane said, "That works for me." Callie had a feeling it didn't. He'd been friendly at school and, unlike Mitch, he seemed to understand when to back off. He must have sensed this was one of those times.

That afternoon Callie saw Mrs. Hobart get into her Mustang wearing her casino dealer outfit. The kids continued to play outside after she'd left. Callie kept checking on and off as it grew dark, and eventually the kids disappeared. She didn't see them go inside because her view of the back porch was blocked, but about the time the kids disappeared from the backyard, the television came on inside the dark house. Deduction? Kids were inside watching TV. Another deduction? There was no adult home, regardless of what the mom had said, because there'd been no lights on until the kids had gone inside. The kids were on their own until their mother got off shift at about 1:30 A.M.

This was wrong.

Callie rebooted her computer, which cast an eerie blue glow as it came to life in the dim room. It only took a moment to find the phone number and address for Child Protective Services in Wesley, and a form to download.

If Denise hadn't mentioned seeing the kids at several fires, and if Callie wasn't going to leave soon, then maybe she would have waited. Or if the mom hadn't lied. But Callie knew from asking at school that it could take weeks for a nonemergency home visit, since there were only two social workers in the county. She wanted the kids to have someone looking out for them after she was gone.

It didn't take long to fill out the form and print it for delivery the next day. She felt crummy, because she honestly didn't want to cause the family trouble. She simply wanted to make sure a couple of kids were not being left uncared for.

CALLIE SPENT MOST of her life in casual clothing, but she could dress up if the occasion called for it. The Crab Feed was a major Wesley social event, ranking right up there with the high school's annual community harvest dance fundraiser. She'd waitressed at the Crab Feed twice during high school as part of her Honor Society community service, and recalled that people had dressed up. So she would.

She slipped into a black knit shift, one of her classiest travel-proof garments. It wasn't clingy, but it did hug her body, skimming over her curves and ending a couple inches above the knee. The wide boatneck gave the dress an Audrey Hepburn look. Callie put on the same string of freshwater pearls she'd worn to Grace's memorial, and slipped her bare feet into black ballet shoes. She wished she had her red ones with her, but they were in storage in California.

Hair. Up? Down? Did it really matter? She wasn't trying to entice the guy. She just didn't want to disgrace herself. Down.

Callie took one last look in the mirror before heading out to the Neon. She forced the corners of her mouth up. Oh, yeah, that looked real.

She tried again. Better. The smile disappeared.

Okay, so she wasn't wild about going to a social event right now, but Dane was a nice guy and he wasn't asking for a commitment. It was just a night out.

The parking lot was full when she arrived at the community center, but she managed to squeeze the Neon into a space between a sedan and the grass at the edge of the lot. She was legal. Almost.

Now all she needed to do was find her date, which proved to be no problem at all, since Dane was the tallest guy in the room. He was standing with a small crowd just inside the door, a drink in his hand, wearing a corduroy blazer and khaki slacks, his sandy hair combed to the side. He looked exactly like an ex-jock. Comfortable in his skin, yet ready for a challenge. She really hoped she wasn't that challenge. He spotted her as soon as she walked in, excused himself from the man he was talking to, a local lawyer she couldn't remember the name of, and went to meet her.

"I paid for your ticket," he said with a half smile.

Callie bit back the "that wasn't necessary." He had asked her, after all, and the tickets were outrageously priced. The money went to charity, though, so Callie had been ready to fork it over. "Thank you," she said.

Dane's gaze traveled over her, but he offered no compliment—aloud, anyway. He let the smile in his eyes do the talking. He approved.

"Would you like a drink?"

"Not yet."

"Then why don't we go sit down? I think you know most of the people at our table," he said, putting a light hand at her waist and directing her past the portable bar, where two guys in the Lions' yellow vests were mixing drinks. "Just a few spousal introductions and you're set."

"Great."

They stopped to talk to several people as they traveled to the table, and Dane's hand settled permanently at her waist.

The microphone whistled and the group turned to see Pete Domingo, the high school principal, adjusting the height of the stand. He cleared his throat, then invited them all to be seated. Dinner would be served by lottery and the last table served would receive a bottle of pricey wine.

"Which means we'll be the second-to-last table served," Dane murmured with a touch of humor as he again put his hand on Callie's waist and guided her through the maze of chairs and large round tables to the center of the room, near the dance floor.

As he said, Callie was already familiar with the three high school teachers there—Mr. Lightfoot, the king of chaos, Mrs. Simms and Mr. Carstensen, aka Phillip, Susan and Rick. They would always be Mr. and Mrs. to her. She smiled and said hello as Dane introduced their respective spouses, then took her seat. Dane pushed in her chair, made certain she was comfortable, his fingers brushing along the bare skin of her shoulders more often than necessary.

The first numbers for the buffet line were announced over the loudspeaker and the people at the table next to Callie stood, laughing and congratulating themselves on choosing the correct seats. Callie moved her chair to give them room to file past, and as she did so her gaze zeroed in on Seth Marcenek two tables away, laughing uproariously. And across the table from him, very preoccupied with a rather beautiful brunette, was Nate. *Oh, good.*

Callie quickly looked away. She should have known he'd be here. The crab dinner was a community-wide social event. She brought her attention firmly back to Mr. Lightfoot, who was telling the story of his recent illness, and feigned rapt interest in blood test screwups.

Did she know the woman sitting with Nate? Was this one of their classmates who had blossomed? If so, she'd done a good job of it. When Callie casually glanced over while arranging her purse on the back of her chair, she saw Nate's dark head tilted toward the woman. When she finished speaking, he laughed, his eyes never leaving hers.

At one time Callie had made Nate laugh and had been on the receiving end of that particular intimate gaze. A long while ago.

A decidedly unwelcome thought came to her. Maybe this woman was the reason he'd backed off at the river. Maybe he was getting involved with someone.

And maybe Callie's stomach shouldn't be tied up in a knot.

Nathan said something to the brunette then, and she smiled and touched his hand. Callie clenched her teeth.

"Wine?"

Dane—*her date,* she reminded herself sternly—was holding the carafe. "Please." She smiled gamely, took a sip and then, as he poured wine into his own glass, she took a larger, more bracing drink.

"So, Callie," Susan Simms said, and all eyes turned to her. Dane's hand slid along the back of her chair and this time his fingers settled lightly on her shoulder.

"You're selling the house? Mrs. Serrano said something to that effect today."

"I just called the Realtor."

"Will you be buying another place here?"

Callie almost laughed, but didn't. "No," she said matter-of-factly. "I'll be leaving." Dane's fingers were now firmly gripping her shoulder, his arm around her as if she was his girlfriend. Which she wasn't.

"I'd hate to see you go," he said with an I'm-as-good-off-the-court-as-I-am-on-the-court confidence that made Callie's hackles rise. Dane was different when he was off school property.

"Oh, I'm kind of looking forward to new vistas," she said as she twisted her chair toward him, making it impossible for him to keep his arm around her shoulders.

"And just when I found a dependable sub," Mr. Lightfoot said as the microphone squeaked behind him, calling another table to the buffet line. Dane met Callie's eyes and once again she saw good-humored laughter, as if he thought she was playing hard to get.

What was it with the guys in this town? Couldn't hook up with the one she wanted, and the others were creeping her out.

NATE HATED TO ADMIT that Seth had chosen his blind date well, but he had. Gina Flores was indeed an attractive, intelligent woman whose company he enjoyed, so it seemed unfair that his attention kept wandering over to where Callie sat with that tall teacher/basketball coach. Nathan therefore made certain that his focus was solely on Gina and their tablemates as they waited for their buffet number to be called. He couldn't say that sparks were flying between him and his date, but she was comfortable to talk to and had a great laugh, soft yet throaty.

She explained what she did in human resources, occasionally looking across the table at Seth, who was doing really bad impersonations, as if wondering how he and Nathan could possibly be related. Sometimes Nathan wondered, too, as his brother butchered his attempt at Jack Nicholson. Everyone could do Jack Nicholson.

The time passed pleasantly enough as they waited forever for their food, except once when he gave in and looked at Callie—and saw the basketball coach sliding his hand possessively along the back of her chair. Nate had never particularly liked Dane Gerard and wondered what the hell Callie was doing here with him.

Okay…maybe he wasn't totally over Callie, but he could fake it until she left town, which according to Joy would be soon, since her cousin, the real estate agent, had just been asked to sell the house.

Their table number got called second to last. Nathan kept his attention on Gina as they went through the line, resisting the urge to watch Dane and Callie. When they sat back down with their plates and started cracking crab, Gina asked why he'd chosen journalism when his brothers were both involved in "less cerebral" occupations. Nathan appreciated the way she phrased the question, making it seem for once as if he was the sane one in the family. Definitely the one with brains. He glanced over at Seth, wearing his beat-up Aerosmith T-shirt under a corduroy blazer, and understood why his brother was getting nowhere with Gina.

"My mom wrote," Nate said, surprising himself with the answer.

"Was she published?"

"Oh, no. Journals. Lots and lots of journals." He'd often sat with her and doodled in his own notebooks as a child, and later, after her death, had started journals of his own. Living in terror that his brothers would find them and blackmail him. Or worse.

Gina smiled and worked the last bits of meat out of a claw. "It's funny how our parents' interests shape our lives. Did you ever consciously decide to be like her and write?"

"Uh…no." He hadn't really thought about the connection before, but yeah, writing did make him feel closer to her.

"She must be proud of you."

"She would have been." He supposed. More so than his father, though, who was raucously entertaining the troops on the other side of the room. "She passed away when I was twelve."

"I'm sorry." Gina focused her soft brown eyes on him. "That might be even more of a reason you pursued it."

"Yeah. Maybe." Again, he'd never thought about that before.

"SO HOW'VE YOU LIKED substitute teaching?" Mr. Lightfoot asked. Callie wondered if he was aware of what a chaotic mess his room was and how a simple seating chart would make a sub's life so much easier. She'd found out from the students that he didn't bother with seating charts. They sat where they wanted, and when they had a sub, they also took on whatever identity they wanted. Juvenile, but apparently amusing to sophomores.

"There's more to it than I'd first anticipated."

Dane laughed. "Well phrased. It's more than baby-sitting."

"So tell us about being a journalist," Mrs. Lightfoot said, leaning closer. "I hear you've traveled all over the world."

"I've been a few places."

"You've written for some well-known magazines. I'm surprised the newspaper isn't taking more advantage of your presence than just those few piddling articles."

"Damned good piddling articles," Dane said.

"Is there some reason you aren't writing more for them?" Mrs. Lightfoot pressed, looking first at Callie, then over Callie's head to where Nathan sat.

Someone had been listening to gossip.

"I have other things to fill my time," she answered, carefully wiping dripping butter off her wrist.

"Like subbing." Mr. Lightfoot chortled as if he'd just told a joke.

Callie smiled weakly, reaching for her water glass, wishing it was gin, when the fire siren sounded, cutting off Mrs. Lightfoot just as she was about to speak. About a dozen pagers went off a split second later. The room erupted into activity as members of the volunteer firefighters sprang into action. Wives and girlfriends exchanged looks. Yet another evening shot.

"A field near the old feed plant," John Marcenek called to the men sitting at another table, before flipping a cell phone shut. Chairs scraped back. One fell over as the guy struggled with it.

Callie abruptly set down her waterglass. The feed plant wasn't that far from her house, just on the other side of the river. Was her little white-haired neighbor going to be there? She pushed her chair back, too, without conscious thought. She didn't know if the social workers had investigated yet, but just in case, she wanted to make sure the little kids weren't at this fire. If they were, she was turning them over to Garrett.

"I'll go with you," Dane said. Callie realized he probably thought she was looking for a story. "We'll take my car," he added.

"No." Callie cut a sideways glance his way as they

followed a group of men out the front door. "I like to have my own transportation." But Dane wasn't put off.

"Suit yourself," he said easily, once again pressing his hand to her waist, but she sidestepped and then walked faster so he couldn't do it again. *Hint, buddy. Take the hint. You're too pushy for me.*

The air smelled of burning sagebrush when they walked out to the dark lot, where pickup trucks and cars with volunteer fire department license plates were pulling out of parking spots. There was an orange glow on the edge of town, across the river from Callie's house.

She got into the Neon and followed several cars across the river, where she parked on the highway above the feed plant. She'd have an excellent view of the action and still be far enough from the fire that the authorities probably wouldn't send her on her way. Other cars parked along the highway, some driven by firefighters, some by people who simply stopped to watch.

Dane pulled his shiny BMW in behind her. Flames shot high from the dead elm trees that had once formed a windbreak around the plant, and two engines were already in position, shooting jets of water onto the trees. Another was attacking the rapidly moving line of fire in the field between the plant and the river.

Smoke rolled over the highway as Callie walked back to Dane's car, where she could get a better look at the small groups of people. He waved his hand in front of his face. "Man, this is nasty."

"One of the side effects of fire," Callie said as she searched for the Hobart children.

Nothing. No children at all. Yet. Most of the people gathering to watch were residents of the housing development above the highway. Callie had seen several of them pull into their driveways and then walk down to the edge of the road.

She turned her attention back to the fire, watching the firefighters spray water on the flames. A truck with a blade was digging a line around the structures. Unlike the previous fire Callie had witnessed, the volunteer force wasn't making much headway. The fire was still relatively small, but vegetation was dry after a month with no rain and the wind kept shifting direction.

A fluorescent-green BLM fire truck rumbled from the highway down the river road to the plant. A second later another followed.

"Bringing in reinforcements," Dane said.

"The plant must abut BLM land." The BLM wouldn't fight a fire on city or county property, but they would stand ready in case the flames spread onto federal land.

Callie once again searched the crowd lining the highway. Still no kids. She was starting to feel better.

NATHAN HAD CAUGHT A RIDE to the fire with his father, getting a free pass to the action. Gina had understood and sent him on his way. Seth had indeed chosen well in the date department. He just hadn't chosen what Nathan really wanted. Nate hated to think about what that was, because once he admitted it, he was going to have to deal with it—until she left town. And then he had a sneaking suspicion he was still going to be dealing with it.

"You all right?" the old man mumbled without looking at him.

"Yeah." But his fingers were unconsciously kneading his thigh. He shoved his hand in his jacket pocket. As soon as they got to the fire, John jumped out of the pickup and headed toward the fire truck, pulling on equipment as he walked.

Garrett stopped next to the pickup in the sheriff's office vehicle. "Shit," he said in a low voice. "They'd better not lose this one." He looked behind him, up toward the highway, where people were already parking, some firefighters, some not. "Keep an eye on Dad. I've gotta do crowd control… Oh, cool. Look who's here."

Nathan could tell from Garrett's tone exactly who was there. Callie. He wondered if Dane was with her. A quick backward glance, and yeah. He was there. Even at this distance Nate could recognize the two of them standing side by side, near Dane's pricey car. But the Neon was parked next to it.

Nathan felt a sense of grim satisfaction. Dane had followed her. They hadn't arrived together.

IT TOOK ALMOST half an hour for the firefighters to get enough of a handle on the blaze to send one of the

BLM trucks back to the bay. The other remained, just in case. An older and heavier John Marcenek was directing the crews. It had taken Callie a while to recognize him, but once she zeroed in on Nate, she'd realized who the man with him was. She did not like that man, pretty much because he made no secret of not liking her.

Denise was also there, geared up and in the center of the action. Callie was impressed at how efficiently she worked, appearing to know exactly what needed to be done and where at every step of the operation.

"Are you going to stay much longer?" Dane asked with a glance at his watch.

That was her cue to agree that the fire had been diverting entertainment, but it was now time to leave. "Afraid so," she said. "Why don't we call it a night?"

Dane raised his eyebrows. "Are you sure?"

"Yeah." Callie smiled up at him, although the smile didn't quite reach her eyes. "Can't help myself. I'm a journalist to the core and I want to be where the action is."

And she didn't want to leave with him.

"Can't fault you there," Dane said. And since it was pretty obvious there would be no good-night kiss or make out session or whatever he'd hoped for, he smiled awkwardly before turning and walking back to his car.

Callie was so damned glad she had the Neon. Dinner

with the group had been…unusual, but she wasn't ready to spend the rest of the evening with Dane.

Single women might be few and far between in Wesley, but she didn't need him all but planting a flag on her and claiming "mine."

CHAPTER TEN

THE FIREFIGHTERS FINALLY secured a perimeter around the abandoned feed plant and then, aided by a wind shift, they began to get the upper hand on the blaze. The smoke now rolled toward town, away from where Nathan and Garrett stood beside the idling BLM truck, but his eyes and nostrils continued to burn. A few yards away, Seth was performing his paramedic duties, treating one of the firemen who'd stepped in a hole and wrenched a knee, and his father was in rare form at the engines, bellowing orders and running his crew.

Garrett suddenly cursed and Nathan turned to see that a number of fire groupies were edging closer. Some of the residents of the small housing development on the hill above the plant, most of whom had been at the Crab Feed, had made their way down to the parking lot and were standing in a scraggly line where sage met gravel.

Callie was there, too, off to the side. It occurred to Nathan that that was how she led her life, observing from the periphery. The basketball coach was nowhere in sight. She hunched her shoulders and wrapped her arms around her middle as he watched, rubbing her palms over her upper arms, her gaze shifting from the fire to the crowd, which was growing rather than shrinking. The night air was sending chills up Nathan's back even though he was wearing a blazer, and Callie only had on a sleeveless black dress. Yet still she stayed, shivering. Why? And it was crazy, but he felt an urge to walk over to her and simply wrap his arms around her, warm her by holding her close. Many years ago he could have done that. It killed him to admit it, but he missed those days.

She glanced over at him then, and for a moment they studied each other across the distance that separated them. He had never known anyone else who could connect with him like she could. As if they could read each other's minds if they tried hard enough.

"I'm pushing the crowd back," Garrett said, breaking into Nathan's thoughts. "Go shoo Callie home." His brother smirked as he spoke, telling Nathan that he'd caught the two of them staring like star-crossed lovers. Shit.

Nathan crossed the distance to her.

"You need to go home. There's the potential for volatile substances to react with the fire."

She twisted her mouth sideways in a dubious expression. "For real? Or are you making that up to get me out of here?"

"Both."

Callie held her ground. "Is the fire manmade?"

"We don't know yet." Nate gestured to where the Neon sat on the highway above the parking lot and asked, "Where's your dinner date?"

"He went home."

"Separate cars?"

"You know me," she said. "Sharing a car is too much of a commitment."

"Why're you here, Cal? All these other people have houses close by." Part of him wondered if she'd come to escape her date. She hadn't appeared to enjoy her companion for the evening as much as he'd enjoyed his.

"I came to see if those little kids next door showed up."

"You're kidding."

She shrugged. "Denise told me she's seen them at other fires and this one is close."

Nate tilted his head. "Do you think they're junior arsonists or something?" he asked, trying to see where she was going with this.

"No. Like I told you before, I don't think anyone is taking care of them at night. I think they do as they please and I think the boy is interested in either fire or firemen."

"So you're gathering evidence?" Or attempting to, since the kids weren't there.

"I'm concerned."

"Just because you haven't seen the grandma—"

"There are no lights on in that place, Nate. Except the television every now and then. And the kids show up at fires."

"So do a lot of people."

"I guess."

"Go home, Callie." She was shivering even worse in her skimpy dress, and there was no reason for her to be there. "The kids aren't here."

"Nate!" Seth sounded uncharacteristically panicked. Nathan stumbled as he turned toward the voice, his injured leg giving out with the unexpected movement. Searing pain shot through his knee, but he didn't stop moving. Garrett raced past him from the direction of the parking lot and Nathan followed as quickly as he could, wincing with each step. Their father was leaning heavily against the fire truck, halfheartedly fighting off Seth and another paramedic.

"Are you all right?" Callie asked from behind Nate. He hadn't realized she was following him.

"Fine," he replied without looking at her.

"Go back to the parking lot, Callie," Garrett commanded when she and Nathan reached the small group of people surrounding his father.

Callie ignored him. "What's wrong with John?" she asked Nathan.

"Blood pressure." He hoped. "Controllable *if* he takes his medication."

"Why *wouldn't* he take it?"

"Makes him irritable," Nathan muttered.

"One would never notice," Callie murmured, as John cursed Seth and the other paramedic, trying to push them back.

"Go home, Callie." Garrett stepped between her and Nathan. "I'll walk you to your car."

"No need," she said through her teeth.

"I insist."

"Call him off," she said to Nathan, then turned and stalked across the lot and up the trail to her car.

"DAMN IT, I'M FINE." John took a few steps toward the rear engine, looking very much as if he was about to wrestle control of the fire crew from his second in command. Nathan took his arm, stopped him cold in spite of his dad outweighing him by a hundred pounds.

"You're not fine," Nate growled. "You're going to the emergency room." His father sent him a baleful look and attempted to snatch his arm away. He failed, which worried Nathan. "You have to go. You'll need a medical release to continue fighting fires after this."

Seth nodded in agreement, quickly backing away from their dad. The air seemed to go out of John Marcenek. His shoulders dropped as the reality of what Nathan had said sank in.

"Dr. Kitras owes me a favor," Garrett said. "We'll see if we can get you in tomorrow, but tonight we're going to the E.R. and making sure everything is okay."

"Whoopee," John muttered, but he started walking toward the passenger side of his truck. There wasn't much else he could do. Garrett opened the door, earning another cranky look, and Nathan got into the driver's seat.

"Seth and I'll be there as soon as we can," Garrett said.

John turned his head as if he didn't hear a word. Nathan started the truck and they drove to the clinic in silence.

The doctor had John checked over before either Garrett or Seth arrived, and pronounced him out of any immediate danger. However, if he didn't stay on his medication, he was looking at a possible heart attack or stroke. Not what John Marcenek had wanted to hear. Nathan called his brothers and they agreed to meet at the house. Their trucks were there when Nate and John pulled up.

Together the three followed their dad into the immaculate kitchen. John had never been particularly tidy before, but apparently retirement did strange things to people.

"You can go home now," he said to Nathan. "I'm going to bed, so one watchdog will be fine." With that he walked down the hall to the room he'd once shared with their mother.

Garrett and Nathan exchanged silent looks, then Garrett went to the cupboard over the refrigerator and pulled down the bottle of Scotch. Nathan shook his head. "Not tonight," he said. "I twisted my leg and I might opt for a painkiller instead."

"This kills pain," Garrett muttered, pouring a shot.

"Yeah. You might want to save some for after you take Dad to see Kitras tomorrow."

"Will do," Garrett said glumly. "How bad's your leg?" The limp was obviously getting worse.

Nathan ran a hand over the thigh, even though it was his knee that had been injured. "It'll be fine. When you have only a few muscles to begin with, it really has an effect when you strain one."

"I guess. Let me know if I need to finagle two appointments tomorrow. I'm sure Kitras will see both of you at once."

"Can't. Too much work to catch up on."

Nathan's leg was throbbing when he got home, but he decided against the bottle of white pills in his medicine cabinet, and followed Garrett's lead. He splashed two fingers of amber liquid over a single ice cube in a crystal glass, then on impulse added another finger. What the hell. This stuff couldn't make him any groggier tomorrow than the conventional painkiller. And it tasted better. He probably should have shared a drink with Garrett, but his brother really would need all of that bottle to deal with their father.

Nate was so thankful right now that Garrett was the brother living next door to their dad.

He picked up a framed photo Seth had given him last Christmas, taken on a father-son fishing trip in Alaska when the brothers had been in their early teens, six months after the death of their mother. They each held a humongous salmon. Garrett was smirking at the camera, looking like the hellion he'd been at the time, and Seth beamed like a puppy dog, the look that hid his natural propensity toward getting into every kind of trouble imaginable, some innocent and some not so much. Nathan looked like the brother who wanted to please. The brother who tried to hold things together in a family that had just lost their mother.

Carelessly, he set the photo on the coffee table and then settled on the sofa, staring across the dark room.

What was going to happen if he decided to leave town? Was it right to leave his brothers to take care of their dad? Would his dad even care if he left?

Why did he feel this urge to move on? Was this how Callie felt? Did she just get the urge, and instead of weighing pros and cons slowly, as he did, simply act on it?

He wasn't that way. He wanted to know what he had available to fall back on. He liked to plan.

He'd heard that that very afternoon Callie had called a real estate agent—Joy's cousin—for a consultation. The wheels were in motion to sell the house, which meant she would probably be leaving town. It wouldn't be long before Callie was out of his life. Out of his thoughts.

Yeah. He really could fake not caring until she left town. No sweat. He took a sip of Scotch, feeling the burn as it hit the areas of his mouth and throat still irritated from smoke inhalation. He didn't mind the burn.

What an evening. He'd started out nervous about going out with a woman, even if it was a lame group date, and had ended up stinking of smoke and going home as alone as he had left. Not that he'd planned to go home with Gina, because as pleasant as it had been talking to her, it wasn't going anywhere. There was no spark. And he'd been thinking about Callie and that freaking basketball coach the entire time. Insane.

Callie made him insane. He sipped again.

He saw a flash of headlights in the window and then heard the sound of an engine turning off. Nathan put the crystal glass to his forehead. He recognized the distinctive knocking noise in the Neon's engine.

"It's open," he called when Callie knocked, adding in an undertone, "Come on in."

She did, pausing for a moment, taking in the scene—Nathan sprawled on the sofa, the drink in his hand.

"How's your dad?" she asked as she closed the door.

"He'd gone off the meds again. I think this time he learned a lesson."

She walked the rest of the way across the room, stopping inches from his toes. He glanced down at his jeans, wondering if she could see the difference between his thighs under the worn fabric. She followed his gaze momentarily before bringing her eyes back up to his face.

"You hurt yourself at the fire."

"I wrenched my knee."

"Can I sit down?"

"It's late."

"It's not even midnight." He didn't invite her to sit, though.

"I heard you put the house on the market."

"I'm in the process. It's time."

"Do you always know when it's time?"

"Always." She picked up the photo he'd left on the coffee table and studied it.

"So, it was time when you left here last?"

She looked up from the photo, obviously uncomfortable. "That was different."

"How?"

"I was reacting to something I didn't understand back then."

"Do you understand it now?"

"I understand it's the way I am. The way I'm wired. My father was the same way—"

"—according to Grace." Nate finished the sentence with her. They'd been over this before, back in high school, only at that time, Callie hadn't thought she was wired the same way as her father. She'd needed to believe then that he hadn't been able to help himself. Now she was telling herself she was the same way, giving herself an excuse to leave whenever she felt the urge. Avoid any kind of commitment.

Maybe she *was* wired the same way as her father. Nathan didn't know. He stared at what was left of his Scotch, which he was now drinking too fast. "So you're just going to spend your life moving from place to place?"

"I guess I am now, once I sell the house." She glanced away, making Nathan wonder if she was nervous about that—having no home base. He couldn't imagine not having one himself. Even if he didn't want one, it seemed to find him, in the form of two brothers and one disapproving father. But it was a form of security. A form Callie would never know, having no family.

"Did they ever figure out what happened to him?" Nathan asked. "Your dad?"

A shadow crossed her features. "No."

Callie carefully set the photo back where she'd found it, then wiped her palms down the sides of her black dress. Their eyes met and once again Nathan felt that silent connection he found with no one else.

"What do you want, Callie? Why do you keep coming here?"

"Is that woman you were with tonight your girlfriend?"

A perfect chance for escape. Nathan didn't take it. Instead, he looked wearily into her beautiful aqua eyes and said, "No. Blind date. How about you?"

"Sucky date. We should have been together, Nate."

His mouth tightened as he looked away. Right. They should be together, then he could fall in love with her again, and then she could leave. Great plan.

"We're driving each other crazy," she said. He couldn't argue with her there. "Why can't we push all this crap aside and simply *be* together while I'm here? You know you feel as drawn to me as I am to you. In some ways it's like we've never been apart in spite of everything that happened."

Nathan got awkwardly to his feet, his knee buckling slightly, and Callie stepped aside, giving him room to move. He limped past her into the kitchen, where only one low-watt bulb burned above the sink. He poured another splash of Scotch over what was left of the ice cube. Warm Scotch, cold Scotch. He didn't care.

"Be together," he said after taking a healthy swallow. "Like being friends…only friends who can't trust each other."

"I will always be up front with you. Before, I didn't know what was happening. I panicked. I thought a clean break would be easiest for both of us. I handled it so poorly, but I was afraid I would give in if I stayed in touch."

And would that have been so bad?

Apparently so.

"How would it be different this time?"

"We both need different things now than we did back then."

"What about sex?" Nathan asked in a low voice. "Is that part of the package?" He reached down with his right hand and absently touched the numb muscles of his thigh, felt the ugly divot, and could not imagine making love to Callie this way.

"The attraction is there and you can't tell me it's not. I think sex would be good for us. In fact, I think we're overdue after what happened the last time. As long as we understand the situation."

Nathan put the glass on the counter with such force that a small amount of Scotch sloshed out, pooling gold on the white counter.

"Listen, Callie. I don't want to have sex with you because it would be good for us or for old time's sake or because you 'care' enough to have sex before you blast out of my life again. I don't want you to make up for the past, and I don't want to be on the receiving end of sympathy."

"Who said anything about sympathy?"

Right. Who had said anything about sympathy? Nathan muttered a curse. "I don't want to have sex because you feel bad about the past. How's that?"

"Very clear," Callie said, her eyes revealing no emotion. "I can't help the way I am, Nate."

"And I can't help the way I am, either." But it sure seemed stupid that at one time they'd been soul mates and now…now this chasm.

"I think you still care about me."

"Even if I did, Callie, I wouldn't do anything about it, because there's no future in it."

"Is that what you're looking for? Is that one of the prerequisites? The guarantee of a future?"

"No. The possibility of a future. With you there isn't even that. I've lost before I start. I won't do that again. I won't waste the time again."

She looked stunned by his last words. She said nothing for a moment, then abruptly turned and walked back through the living room to the front door, where she let herself out. A moment later the Neon pulled away from the curb, leaving Nathan very much alone. Again. Just as he'd been before she'd shown up, but now it felt even worse.

It felt final.

I WON'T WASTE THE TIME.

Callie parked at the curb in front of her house five minutes later, Nate's harsh words circling through her mind.

Just forget about him. You can't keep beating your head on the wall. Just give it up.

She was so preoccupied talking herself down that she completely missed the guy sitting in the shadows on her porch steps. When he moved she jumped a mile, then went into instant defense mode before she recognized him, and even then she didn't drop her guard.

"Mitch. You scared me." She kept her distance as she pressed a hand against her chest in an effort to still her hammering heart.

"Enjoy your evening with the coach?"

"It was an evening." What was going on? Why was this kid here and what did he want? No, it was obvious what he wanted. To what lengths would he go to get it?

"And then you went to see Marcenek. Think Coach knows about that?"

Callie's eyes grew round. "You were following me?"

Mitch shrugged. "So what's wrong with me? I mean, if you're seeing two guys, why not three?"

Callie drew herself up. "Because the third one is too immature and arrogant for my tastes."

And he was also a big kid. Much stronger than she was and probably a lot faster.

"You'd better go now, Mitch…before you *disturb the neighbors!*" Callie shouted the last words, noticing that Alice's windows were open and the television was on. The Hobart house was as dark as always.

Mitch smirked at her and stepped forward, but Alice's porch light snapped on and he jumped back. Callie could see his face, and what she saw unnerved her. Cold determination.

"Leave," she told him.

Alice opened her door and peered out.

"Hey, Alice," Callie called, her eyes fixed on Mitch's face. "So help me, I'll have her call the cops if you don't get your ass out of here."

"Are you all right, Callie?" Alice called.

"I will be in a few seconds," she said through gritted teeth as she stared the kid down. Mitch gave her a look of hatred and stormed off to his car. He fired up the engine and pulled away from the curb with a screech of tires.

Alice came out onto her porch in a wild floral print robe, her hand over her chest. "Are you all right, Callie? Who was that?"

Callie crossed her arms over her chest, hugging herself as she watched the taillights disappear around the corner. "Mitch Michaels."

"Really!"

"Yes." And now what did she tell Alice? That she was seeing another much more intimidating side of this kid that wasn't nearly as charming as the one she'd shut down at school? "It was nothing, Alice. He's just a little persistent."

Even across the distance that separated them, Callie could see her neighbor's shock.

"Trust me, I haven't encouraged him. I, uh, should be getting into the house."

"Are you sure you're all right?" Alice asked in a dubious voice.

"Oh, yes. Everything will be fine now. Good night, Alice."

"Good night."

Callie went into the house, grabbed the phone book and looked up the number for the sheriff's office dispatch. Thankfully, the deputy who called back a few minutes later was not Garrett.

She briefly explained that Mitch Michaels had followed her that evening and had been waiting for her at her house, where he'd behaved in a threatening manner. The deputy sounded rather pleased with the situation, making Callie wonder if he had something against the rich Michaels family or if he'd had dealings with Mitch before and was looking to take the kid down.

"I'll have a talk with him tonight if I can locate him," the deputy promised. "Tomorrow, if I can't. If he persists, then you'll have to consider taking stronger measures."

"Should I have reason to believe he's going to persist?" Callie asked.

"Your guess is as good as mine, but just in case, keep that in mind."

How very helpful, Callie thought as she hung up the phone. *Your guess is as good as mine.*

She locked all the doors and windows and then went to bed, more creeped out by the situation than she wanted to admit.

CHAPTER ELEVEN

NATHAN WAS JUST OPENING the garage door to go to work when Garrett pulled up to the curb in the sheriff's office SUV. Curious, since this looked a lot like an official visit, Nathan walked toward him. Garrett got out of the car and met him halfway up the drive.

"I wanted you to hear this from me, rather than through the very efficient grapevine."

Nathan didn't like the expression on his brother's face. "Hear what?"

"Callie made a complaint against Mitch Michaels. I guess he was following her last night. Followed her here, in fact, and then confronted her at her house."

Rage unlike anything Nathan had ever felt before exploded inside him. He turned and started back toward the garage without another word.

"Don't do anything stupid, Nate."

He turned back. "Me? I'm the calm, quiet brother. Remember?"

Garrett looked heavenward for an instant. "Just make

sure you stay that way. We had extra patrols driving by her place last night. She was safe."

"You didn't go talk to the little asshole?"

"We did. A deputy found him in the café with some friends who swore he'd been with them all night."

"So Callie just imagined it."

"Exactly."

Nathan ground his teeth. "Well, perhaps I'll help Mitch imagine a few things today."

"Watch yourself. If you assault him, it won't endear you to your boss and it won't keep Callie safe."

Oh, yeah. He'd watch himself. "I don't care if Callie isn't your favorite person," Nathan said to his brother, "you continue to make damned sure nothing happens to her, understand?"

"I understand," Garrett repeated wearily. "Just don't do anything to that kid. Let us handle it."

Nathan released a long breath. "I'll try," he muttered. It was the best he could do. He wasn't making any promises.

He spent the morning in his office with his door closed, debating how he was going to continue to work for Vince Michaels when he wanted nothing more than to eviscerate his son. And there was another asshole son coming up through the ranks.

Nate had cooled down slightly by the time Mitch showed up for his intern hours that afternoon—enough so that he didn't grab the kid by the lapels and slam him up against a wall. His burning rage had turned into more of a cold, controllable anger.

"I'd like to talk to you." Nathan gestured for the young man to step into his office. There was no doubt in his mind that Mitch knew why. He smirked and walked by him with his distinctive rolling swagger.

Nathan closed the door and leaned back against his desk, folding his arms over his chest as he studied the kid, who stared back insolently. Finally Nathan spoke, slowly and clearly.

"If you go near Callie McCarran, or any other woman, for that matter, I'll cut your nuts off."

Shock crossed Mitch's face, replaced almost immediately by the smirk. This kid felt so freaking safe.

"I'm also reporting Katie's concerns from last spring."

"Big deal."

"Last I heard, med school doesn't encourage the admission of students with histories of blatant sexual harassment and stalking."

Mitch's face went purple. He didn't wait to hear another word, but instead wrenched the door open and stormed out, then out the front door. A few seconds later, Nathan heard rubber peeling in the parking lot. He had a feeling that nothing good was going to come of this, but if he had it to do all over again, he wouldn't change a thing.

CALLIE WAS ON THE front porch showing the repairman the window screens she wanted replaced when the county vehicle pulled to a stop in front of the Hobart house. The pink Mustang was there, so the mom was home. Callie wondered if CPS had warned her they were coming, or if they simply swooped in unannounced.

Either way, she felt better knowing someone was finally checking into the situation. She hated sticking her nose into other people's business, but the Hobart kids couldn't continue staying alone at night. It was wrong. Flat out wrong.

After lining the repairman out, she went inside and finished up her last article for the paper on the twice-retired woman who had then got her teaching certificate and was now teaching kindergarten even though she was in her mid-seventies. It had been a fascinating interview, since the woman had done so very much. Having never married or had children, she spent her life following whatever career path interested her at the time.

Although she didn't foresee teaching kindergarten anywhere in her future, Callie identified with the woman. The thought was surprisingly dissatisfying.

There were some weird things going on in her brain these days.

Callie paced through Grace's nearly empty house, feeling almost as empty inside. At every other point in her life when issues had sprung up, she'd been quite satisfied to move along, leaving them behind. Maybe she'd reached a stage where she realized walking away wasn't a solution, but rather a cover-up.

Callie finished the article and e-mailed it to the *Star,* then shut off her computer. She was in the kitchen making tea when there was a knock on the front door. Mrs. Hobart. Through the gap in the front window curtains, Callie could see her standing on the porch.

In spite of all her instincts telling her not to answer the door, that this could not in any way be good, Callie sucked it up and unlatched the door lock.

"You bitch." She had barely opened the door when Mrs. Hobart, hands planted firmly on her nonexistent hips, let fly. "What in the hell were you thinking, calling CPS on me? *You bitch!"* She repeated it in case Callie hadn't received the message the first time.

"I thought your kids were out at night without supervision. That the house was dark when you were gone, and they were home."

"My mom has an apartment in the basement. That's where the kids spend their evenings. I leave the lights off upstairs to save money. Maybe you don't have to worry about electric bills, *inheriting* like you have, but I have to support my mom and my kids."

Callie felt the blood rising in her cheeks. She had no way to see basement lights. She hadn't even known the house had a basement. There were no windows, no door. Nothing.

"And now you know what you've done? You've

opened the door for my asshole ex-husband to come in and try to take the kids from me."

"I, uh—"

"If—and I mean it from the bottom of my soul—he gets custody of my kids, then you are going to so deeply regret ever putting your nose in my business…."

Callie swallowed, knowing there was nothing she could say to defend herself that she hadn't already said.

"I'm sorry. I was concerned about your kids."

Mrs. Hobart sneered. "Well, maybe you'd better be concerned about your ass from now on." And with that she stormed down the sidewalk and out the gate, which banged shut behind her.

Callie watched the woman go, her face feeling first hot and then cold. Her heart beat in a slow, heavy rhythm.

She walked back into the house and closed the door, leaning her forehead against the cool glass.

Nate had told her to be careful. But she had truly believed there was a problem in the family, that the kids were being neglected—and she had reacted at gut level. Why? Why had the idea of those kids being left alone struck such a cord?

Yes, her own childhood must play a part, but she'd accepted her childhood.

Or thought she had.

Of course she had.

Her head was throbbing. Was there anything in her life that wasn't screwed up? Anything at all?

"WHAT'S UP?" Nathan said into his cell phone as he saved his files on the computer.

"Want to grab a beer?" Garrett asked. He'd taken their father in for a follow-up physical late that afternoon.

"Anything I need to be mentally prepared for?"

"No. Better than I'd hoped, but Dad's mad."

"The Supper Club or Fuzzy's?"

"Fuzzy's."

Nathan was still at the office. The only person at the office, since normal people were home with loved ones, or out and about. "Be there in ten."

He was actually there in five. Garrett was waiting at a table with a beer in his hand and two unopened bottles in the middle of the table.

"Did you call me from here?"

"Yeah." Garrett nudged a beer toward him. Nathan took it and drank deeply. Fuzzy's was a classic dark bar. No live music, just a dated selection on a jukebox that no one bothered to play. No waitresses. No bar food. People who came to Fuzzy's were there to drink. They also tended to mind their own business.

"What's the deal with Dad?"

Garrett launched into a bunch of medicalese from which Nathan deduced what they already knew—that if John stayed on the medication, he'd be fine. If he went off, he wouldn't be. "Well, to make a long story short," Garrett concluded, tilting the top of his beer bottle in Nathan's direction, "he can't be on the firefighting squad anymore. He can do logistics, but he can't physically fight the fires."

"That's a hell of a lot better than the alternative."

"Not to Dad. All or nothing." Garrett looked over his shoulder at the bar, then back again. "Want to move into the rental?"

"Oh, yeah. Dad and me living side by side. Good idea. Like his stress level isn't high enough right now."

"Just thought I'd throw it out there," Garrett said morosely.

"I wouldn't last a week."

His brother peeled a strip off his label. It twisted into a curlicue. He let it fall and pulled off another.

"Besides…" Nathan said slowly, "…if Dad really is all right…I don't know if I'm even going to be around."

Garrett's chin popped up. "Why's that?"

"You remember Suzanne, the woman I worked with in Seattle? She called me a while back. There was a job at her paper, but I didn't apply. The next one that opens up, I will."

"You're going back to Seattle?"

"Well, it isn't like I'm going to get blown up twice. That was kind of a freak thing, you know."

"Do you know what a miracle it was that the editorial job opened up here in Wesley when it did? That you had the skills to take over?" Garrett stopped peeling and took a drink.

"Yeah. I do."

"And now that you've done the impossible, landed a journalism job in your hometown, you're throwing it away."

"I can't keep working for Vince Michaels and I don't feel as if I belong here anymore."

Garrett stared at him, his bottle poised in midair. "I can understand about Vince," he finally conceded. "But wait a few weeks, see what happens."

"I still feel like it's time to move on to something else. I'd rather write than edit."

Garrett's eyes narrowed. "Is it because of Callie? Are you following her when she leaves? Because if you are, it's the stupidest move you—"

"No." Nathan cut his brother off. "I have no idea where she's going or what she's doing." And he wished he didn't care. "Maybe having her around made me think a little more, but she's not the reason."

Garrett clearly didn't believe him. Well, Nate wasn't going to justify his decisions with his brother.

"When you came back here, Dad was happy," Garrett finally said.

"I saw him doing those back handsprings across the lawn."

"He was happy." Garrett drained the rest of his beer, then held up two fingers and the bartender nodded.

Bringing over two more, the guy didn't even bother

to pick up Garrett's empty. Nathan was only about a quarter of the way into his first one.

"Speaking of Callie, she called CPS on the Hobarts."

"You're kidding." Nathan put his bottle down. "Any idea what came of it?"

"Officially, no. Unofficially, they made a home visit. The kids tend to run around the neighborhood, but they have a grandmother who lives with them in a basement apartment. That's where they spend their evenings. Or where they're supposed to spend their evenings. The thing is, they have adult supervision."

"Anybody actually see the grandma?" Because he knew Callie didn't believe she existed.

"Interviewed her. She doesn't get out much and…" Garrett shook his head. "Callie can't see the basement door from her house when she's spying."

Nathan took a long pull. So there really was a grandma. Callie had spent all that time worrying for nothing. He wondered how she was handling it. And he was also concerned about the possible ramifications.

"Do the Hobarts know it was her?"

"I think it won't be too hard for them to figure it out."

"No." Nathan cupped his hand around his beer, hoping they didn't enact some kind of hill justice. Why had Callie been so certain those kids weren't being cared for? "Any more uplifting news?"

"I thought it was good news that the kids were being taken care of and that Callie was wrong."

"You like the Callie was wrong part the best."

"Listen, she screwed you over royally. You went into a funk for months. Then you ended up getting your leg nearly blown off."

"Why do you blame Callie for that?" Nathan asked quietly. Had his brothers figured out that when he'd first taken the reporter job, he'd been trying to be more dynamic? Trying to be that guy who would impress the Callies of the world? Was he that transparent?

"Never mind."

"No." Nathan put his bottle down with a thump. "Explain."

Garrett shook his head. "Sorry. Got carried away. I'd better get home to the parental unit," he said, after finishing his beer.

"Better you than me," Nathan muttered, pulling out his wallet and flipping a few bills onto the table.

CALLIE WOKE to the smell of smoke wafting in through her bedroom window. It took her a minute to identify the odor as she fought her way to consciousness, and then, when she opened her eyes and saw flickers of orange light reflecting off the window glass, she shot out of bed.

Her back fence was on fire.

She ran out of the house barefoot, wearing only the gym shorts and T-shirt she'd slept in, and cranked on the garden hose, pulling it across the dark lawn. She was almost to the flames when the hose suddenly stopped uncoiling, yanking her back as she hit the end. Crap.

"Fire!" she screamed as she ran toward the house and her phone. "Alice! Fire!" A light snapped on in the house to her left, and then in the one behind her. Callie dashed onto her porch and through the kitchen. She snatched up her cell phone off the coffee table and punched in 911. When the operator answered, Callie gave her address, and told him there was a fire in the alley, as she once again went out the back door. The fire siren went off and she could see her neighbor across the alley stringing hoses together. The old cedar boards of her shed were burning hot. Callie turned her hose on and started spraying it down so that it wouldn't catch fire, too.

Her throat was dry and her heart hammered. There was only one way a cedar fence would end up ablaze in the middle of the night. Someone had set it on fire.

CHAPTER TWELVE

THE SIREN YANKED NATHAN up out of bed, followed almost immediately by a phone call from Garrett.

"Someone torched Callie's fence," his brother snapped. Nathan's pulse jerked. "The fire crew just got here."

"Is she okay?" he asked as he juggled the phone while pulling on a T-shirt and then ramming his feet into his running shoes.

"Yeah."

He slapped the phone shut and went out the side door to the garage, shoving it in his pocket as he walked to the small truck. He got inside and started the ignition in one movement.

Blood pounded in his temples as he drove the ten blocks to Callie's. He pulled to a stop on the opposite side of the street from her place, parked facing the wrong direction and jumped out of the truck. He crossed the street and skirted the house at a frustratingly slow and painful, limping jog. A single engine sat in the alley. The fire was out and people were gathered close by, talking to Garrett. Callie stood next to her back step, apart from the crowd, staring at what was left of her fence.

Nathan immediately went through the side gate, his only thought to make sure she was all right. He was almost to her when her gaze suddenly jerked sideways toward him. She did not look happy to see him.

For a moment she simply stared at him, slightly shell-shocked, and then she tilted her chin at a defiant angle. "Are you here to waste your time?" she asked.

"Shut up, Callie." He wrapped her in his arms, not caring if she felt his twisted leg through his sweats as her thighs pressed against his. Not caring about anything except that she was safe. Callie stiffened for a moment, and then with a small exhalation, she melted into him. He buried his nose in her hair. She smelled like wood smoke, felt warm and alive. He was so damned grateful.

"Somebody lit my fence on fire," she whispered against his neck.

"I can see that," Nathan replied gently, his arms tightening even more.

"They stacked trash next to it and lit it." Her fingers gripped his shirt as she spoke.

Son of a bitch. He truly wished she'd kept her nose out of Hobart business. "Have you talked to Garrett yet?"

Callie shook her head against his chest.

As footsteps approached, Nathan lifted his head to see his brother with a stern expression on his face. Callie cleared her throat.

"I'm okay," she said as she stepped back, out of his embrace.

I'm not.

But Nathan let go.

"THIS IS SERIOUS," Garrett said, his tone matching his words. Callie had the oddest feeling he was more concerned about Nate being with her than the fire.

"No shit," Nate shot back. "Have you talked to the Hobarts?"

"I will. The kids were in the alley."

"By themselves?" Callie asked sarcastically.

"The old lady has trouble getting around. She pretty much stays nested in that apartment." Garrett shifted his weight into cop stance. "I wanted to talk to you first."

"Not much to tell," Callie said, feeling Nate move closer to her. He didn't touch her, but he was there. "I woke up and smelled smoke. The hose wouldn't reach the fire, so I called 911."

"Do you know of any reason someone might do this? Any hostile contact with anyone?"

Wow, if he'd asked that after Grace's memorial, she would have had quite a list. But right now she only had one.

"Mrs. Hobart came to see me. Told me I was making it possible for her ex to gain custody," Callie said stonily. All because of her knee-jerk reactions. "She was very upset."

"When was this?"

"Today."

Garrett put his hands on his belt. "Okay. Just so you know, there'll be extra patrols through this area for a few days."

Callie bit her lip. She was probably going to see if the motel had a room. "I—"

"Great," Nathan interjected.

"Lock everything. I'll be in contact tomorrow."

"I'm staying with her tonight." Nate met his brother's eyes.

Garrett nodded, then glanced back at the smoldering remains of the fence. "Good idea," he said expressionlessly. "I'll see you two tomorrow."

Nate touched Callie's shoulder. "Let's go inside."

He led the way into the house through the back door.

Callie stopped in the kitchen, which looked so stark now that she'd sent almost everything to charity. "Nate…I…" She halted. She what?

Nate didn't give her time to waffle. "Do you want to come to my house or have me stay over?"

"Your place," she said. "I want to get away from here." When in doubt, run.

"I'll wait while you get whatever you need."

All Callie needed was her purse, a few personal items and a change of clothes, which she shoved into her day pack. "I'll follow you," she said once they were outside.

"Fine." Unlike Dane, he apparently didn't mind if

she kept her freedom. He got into his small truck, which was facing the wrong way, and did a U-turn in the street. Callie followed him to his house, where she parked at the curb. Why was he doing this? Friendship? Guilt? Something more?

Nate stood and waited for her in the bright light of the garage, then, his hand against the small of her back, he guided her into the house.

"You want something to drink?" he asked once they were inside. Callie glanced around at the kitchen, having seen it only once before. It was a man's space, with buff-colored walls, dark cabinets, brushed chrome appliances. A few dishes on the drain board, a newspaper on the table, but other than that, everything in its place.

"Just a glass of water."

He filled a blue highball glass with ice water from the fridge and then poured himself two fingers of Laphroaig. He held up the bottle. "You sure?"

She took a sip of water. "I'm sure. I don't think alcohol will help. I don't know if anything will help. Damn, Nate. They lit my fence on fire."

He lifted the whisky, hesitated, then set the glass back on the counter untouched. Callie took another swallow of water, then she, too, put her glass on the kitchen island that stood between them.

"Why'd you come?" she asked. After their last conversation, he'd been the last person she'd expected to see.

"Garrett called me."

"He must have told you I was okay."

Nathan let out a long breath. "I had to come."

"Why?"

"Because regardless of everything, I care. All right?"

"All right," she repeated, as she tried to make sense of her jumbled thoughts. He cared. He wouldn't let her near him, but he cared.

"It's just that there are some things we have trouble with," Nate said.

"Like talking? We never used to have that problem."

"Maybe something happened," Nate replied darkly.

Callie let her chin dip toward her chest. Something had happened all right. "Since I've come back," she said, "I've been pretty universally despised by those who knew me way back when."

"I—"

She held up her hand to cut him off. "I'm not saying I didn't deserve it, but I never meant to hurt anyone with the things I did. And now..." The intensity of his expression caused words to momentarily escape her. She swallowed. "Now..." She tried to form the words, tried to make some sense of what had happened. To digest the fact that someone hated her enough to risk burning down a neighborhood. To keep from being affected by the way he was staring at her.

"If you start crying..."

He sounded both gruff and desperate. Callie couldn't

help herself. Nate cursed and moved around the island as she wiped the back of her wrist under her eyes. She thought he was going to hold her again, let her get his shirt all wet.

Instead he took her teary face in his hands and kissed her. Deeply, his fingers threading through her hair, making her want to melt into him even though their bodies were a good ten inches apart.

It was crazily erotic to have him holding her face, with only their mouths touching. He showed no signs of ending the kiss anytime soon, but Callie needed more. She wanted to feel him against her. She reached for him, trying to press closer, but he ended the kiss, taking hold of her wrists and confusing the hell out of her. He released her and backed away, slowly dropping his hands, his expression oddly unreadable.

Callie stared at him, not understanding what had just happened. Finally she asked, "Are you doing to me what I did to you?" It was the only explanation she could come up with.

"No."

She almost wished he'd said yes. "Stop playing this game, Nate. You say you don't want to waste time with me, then you show up like a knight errant. You kiss me like that and then back off. I've had one hell of an evening. I don't need this on top of it."

"I'm not doing this to hurt you, Callie."

That was the last straw. *Not doing this to hurt her.*

"Then what's the deal, Nate? What is wrong with two people, two freaking lonely people, because I know you're lonely—I recognize the signs—giving each other some comfort? I did an awful thing to you, but I was eighteen. You're thirty." She let out a shuddering breath. "If you're not doing this to purposely hurt me, then I'd like to know what the hell the deal is."

He didn't answer, so Callie persisted, partially sobbing as she said, "Tell me!"

"You want to know what the deal is?" he answered, suddenly angry. "The deal is that I all but blew my leg off a while ago. I used to be whole but part of me is pretty damned ugly now and I'm still trying to come to terms with it, okay? How's that for a deal?"

For a moment Callie simply stared at him, trying to process what he'd just told her. Then she tilted her head. "Well, at least you're talking to me," she said matter-of-factly. But she was shocked. Her eyes went to his thighs, trying to see…whatever.

"You want to see?" he dared her.

"Yeah." Her eyes came back up and what she saw in his face belied his challenging tone. "If you can handle it," she added, knowing those few words would guarantee he'd follow through. He was, after all, a guy.

Nathan popped the buttons on his jeans and pushed them down, letting them drop around his running shoes.

Callie felt sick as she studied what was left of his right leg. She couldn't look away, not after goading him into showing her. So she did her best to keep a clinical expression as she took in the long, jagged scars, shiny white with pink edges, twisted over the remaining muscles of his leg, a divot missing from his quadriceps and an oddly shaped calf where the muscles had been stitched together around missing tissue. The still-angry burn scars on his calf and ankle. Once again she felt tears welling, thinking of what he had gone through, but did her best to hold them back.

Silently, Nathan lifted his black T-shirt to show similar jagged scars on the right side of his torso. She simply shook her head, unable to find the words. He dropped the shirt back down, then leaned to hoist his jeans up over his ruined leg.

"How?"

"Shrapnel from an explosion."

"Shrapnel," Callie repeated solemnly. "Of course. I should have known." She sent him a sharp look. "Have you been living some kind of double life?"

He shifted his weight. "I worked as an investigative reporter when I was in Seattle. This was my first investigation and ended up being my last. I arranged to meet a contact in a sting operation. Instead I got set up. My partner and I were lucky. It was an incendiary bomb. We should've been killed."

"Your partner? How is he?"

"She. Suzanne Galliano. She was behind me. She got only a few burns from falling material and one minor shrapnel wound to the face. She's still working in the Seattle area. I spent quite a bit of time in the hospital because of the threat of infection, then eventually came here to finish healing. The *Star* editor job opened up while I was here, and I took it."

"Why didn't you tell me any of this?"

"I don't talk about it." Nathan stared out the dark kitchen window. A moment passed and it became obvious he wasn't going to talk anymore about it now.

"Nate…"

"Maybe we should call it a night." He didn't wait for her reply, but picked up her pack where she'd set it at the base of the island, and limped out of the kitchen. Callie considered staying right where she was, but what would that accomplish?

She found him waiting at the end of the hall. He opened a door and set the pack inside. Callie didn't obediently step into the room and close the door, even though she could tell just how badly he wanted her to do that. Instead she reached out to lightly run her fingertips over his T-shirt, where it hid the shrapnel scars. His abdomen tightened.

"Is this the only reason you won't sleep with me?"

"No." The word came out without any hesitation, and hurt a hell of a lot more than it should have.

Okay. Game over. She couldn't take another minute on the emotional seesaw. Not tonight anyway.

Callie reached into the room to pick up her pack, and then retraced her steps back down the hall.

You are so flipping used to rejection. Occupation—writer, remember?

But this wasn't an article.

Nate didn't say a word until she reached the kitchen. "Where are you going?"

"None of your business."

"Stop the drama, Callie."

She rounded on him. "No drama. I'm going to a motel for tonight."

He sucked in a breath. "Stay." She stared at him. "Please stay."

"Why are you doing this?"

He pushed both hands into his hair in a gesture of frustration. "Because I'm afraid, all right?"

HE COULDN'T BELIEVE he'd just said that.

Callie still stared at him, probably wondering for the tenth time that evening why he was such a jerk. And then she swallowed and said, "Me, too."

Nathan drew in a slow breath. "What are you afraid of?"

"That I'm going to leave this town with you still hating me."

Oh, man. "I don't hate you, Callie. I just don't know what making love to you would accomplish."

"Healing," she said softly.

"Healing what?"

"Me. I think I need some healing."

"Okay." He didn't ask for clarification. If she needed healing, then she did. And damn, in spite of everything, he wanted to help her to do just that. He took a couple slow steps forward, bringing them almost toe to toe, but he didn't reach out for her, as much as he wanted to.

"Have you made love to anyone since the…explosion?"

"Yes."

Callie waited.

"She was a nurse…. My nurse."

"Oh."

"Kind of a mercy thing, I think."

Callie hooked her fingers in the waistband of his jeans, putting his manhood on instant alert.

"The relationship didn't last long," he added.

She tugged and he stepped forward.

"So you haven't made love with anyone who wasn't in the medical profession. Someone who isn't used to traumatized body parts?"

"Uh…no."

"I think you should do that. I think you would feel better."

"Maybe," he conceded.

"I may not be able to offer you a future, but I can offer you a very pleasant here and now."

Nathan figured he had two seconds of sanity left. Maybe three, max. He really had to—

"Take off your shirt," Callie said against his mouth before rolling away so that he could actually do as she asked. "I'll take care of the briefs."

After that they didn't talk. Callie explored, touching Nathan's body in the way he'd fantasized about as a kid, with her hands, her lips. She was hesitant when her fingers skimmed over his scarred torso, so she explored him with her mouth instead.

"Is this okay?" She traced her tongue over the sensitive skin between the scars, making him swell almost to the bursting point.

He closed his eyes and nodded. "Fine. It feels fine."

He rolled over on top of her, before she could get to his leg. He was still sensitive about the leg. "I haven't made love to anyone in over a year."

"So you're saying—"

He managed to crack a smile. "If the first time is quick—" he touched his forehead to hers "—I'll make up for it the second time."

"I don't know, Nate. You're older now. Are you sure you're up to two in a row?"

"Oh, I'm up all right." And there'd be no teenage jitters getting in the way tonight.

She pulled his lips down to hers, kissing him aggressively. Making him wonder how long it had been since she'd had a lover. "How about number three?"

"That would be the one that happens before number four," he said roughly.

She laughed. This felt good. Playful. Not overly serious. "I like the way you think."

THEY DIDN'T MAKE IT to number four. The minds were willing, but the flesh was weak. At least until light started spilling in through the windows and Callie reached over for Nate.

He pulled her up on top of him, guiding himself into her, and they made love slowly, one last time. It had to be the last time. Callie could lose herself in the darkness, pretend that making love was all about the here and now, which it was, but making love to Nate in the daylight, watching the reaction in his eyes, feeling him build to climax, his fingers curved around her waist as she rode him…that was different. It was harder to keep the feelings in check.

Damned light.

Callie collapsed against him after they came, then she rolled off.

"And reality comes rushing in," Nathan said, watching her as she put space between them before she turned onto her side, propping her head on her hand. Her hair fell into her eyes and Nathan gently brushed it back.

"How do you feel?"

"Like I love making love to you," she said matter-of-factly.

"For today."

"For as long as I'm here."

He stared down at her, then brought his hand up to tangle in her hair, cupping the back of her head, wanting to pull her onto his chest and kiss her. Then maybe go for number five.

Instead he moved his hand from her hair to gently touch her face. "Promise me one thing, Cal."

"What?" she whispered warily.

"Don't disappear on me, okay? If you're scared, tell me. I'll back off. Just…don't leave."

Callie smiled. It wobbled slightly, but it qualified. "All right," she said, her voice huskier than usual. "I told you I'd be up front with you, so, yeah. I promise."

CHAPTER THIRTEEN

CALLIE HAD BEEN HOME for only a few minutes when there was a knock on the door. She was sore in interesting places, and crossing the living room brought back flashes of the night before. Healing sex with Nate had turned out to be amazing sex.

And now his disapproving older brother stood on her porch.

Normally she wouldn't have been that wild to see Garrett, but today she hoped he had some information on the fire. She invited him in and closed the door behind him. "Would you like some coffee or something?" All she had was instant, since she'd gotten rid of the coffeepot, but cops were supposed to be used to substandard coffee.

"No, thanks. I came to ask a few questions." He was studying her as if she'd committed the crime herself. "Have you had any more dealings with Mitch Michaels since you called Dispatch about him?" he asked sternly.

Callie's eyes widened as she realized what he was getting at. "Do you mean he's the one?"

"Have you had any dealings with him since then?"

"None." Garrett made a note. "Is he the guy who burned my fence?" she repeated.

"The boy next door saw someone that fit the description."

"The Hobart boy?"

"The same. So I asked around and a couple of people two blocks over mentioned a car similar to his parked in their alley at a time that would correspond with the fire."

"What happens now?"

"We'll question him."

Callie put a hand on either side of the base of her neck as she digested what Garrett was telling her. "How sure are you?"

For a second she didn't think he was going to answer, then he said, "I'm sure," before he started toward the door.

"Let me know what happens, will you?"

"Yeah." Garrett's mouth worked for a moment, as if he had something else to say and was trying to hold it back.

"Yes, I left Nate in one piece," she said. Satisfied and exhausted. In that order.

Garrett's eyes narrowed. "I don't think he always makes the best decisions where you're concerned."

"They're his decisions to make."

"Do you know about…" His eyes remained hard as his voice trailed away.

"The bomb. Yes. I know." So there.

"I think he took that job to impress you."

Callie drew back. "No way."

"You dumped him because he was boring, so he decided to become un-boring."

"I did not dump him because he was boring."

"That's not how he saw it. He saw it as not measuring up. Not even being worthy of a phone call."

"You're…you're not putting this guilt trip on me, Garrett."

"I don't have anything against you personally. I just don't want to see you tie my brother in knots again."

It was all Callie could do not to slam the door after Garrett had left. She didn't believe that Nathan took that job because of her. If he was proving he wasn't boring, the only person he had to convince was himself.

NATHAN SETTLED AT his desk, wishing he could spend the day with Callie, and knowing that was impossible, even if his work schedule would allow such a thing. Which it wouldn't.

Callie wanted him to be there for her, but he didn't think she'd counted on the intensity of feelings between the two of them the night before. What she'd had in mind was comforting sex between friends. Sex to help her forget the fire. Sex to make Nate feel better about himself. She probably hadn't counted on mind-numbing sex. Even Nate had been surprised, and he'd wanted Callie for a long, long time. He just hadn't been able to admit it to himself.

His cell phone rang before he'd managed to address even one of the multitudes of tasks awaiting his attention. He flipped it open.

"Finally turned your phone on?" Garrett asked snidely, making Nathan believe that his brother knew exactly why he'd turned it off last night.

"Do you know something about the fire?"

"I think Mitch Michaels started it, but I don't know why he did it last night instead of when Callie turned him in. Maybe he just needed time to stew."

Oh shit. "How sure are you?"

"On a scale of one to five…six.'

Nathan brought his hand up to his forehead. "I ripped him a new asshole when I found out that he'd tried to intimidate Callie."

"And that would have been…?"

"Two days ago." Nathan had no problem believing the kid was that vindictive. "He hit on little Katie here at work last spring and I threatened him with a harassment charge. He backed off, but when I found out he was at it again…"

"You kinda lost it."

"Yeah."

"And Callie was involved."

"Yeah," Nate answered flatly, in a you-want-to-make-something-of-it? tone. "How do you know it's him?"

"Eyewitnesses. Two saw him and one is over the age

of eighteen, so he's a little more reliable than my other witness. I've found three people who saw his car parked in an alley a few blocks away at the time of the fire."

"Have you questioned him?"

"Sure have. Just one problem."

"What's that?"

"His frigging family gave him an alibi."

Nathan sat straighter in his chair. "So what are you going to do?"

"I'm going to continue to investigate, see how much evidence I can put together."

"Get something concrete, will you?" There were too many small things that a big-name attorney could seize upon in a circumstantial case—and Nathan could almost see the lawyers lining up outside Vince Michaels's office door.

"Oh, I'll do my best," Garrett said. "I've been wondering about other *incidents*.... I have some people to talk to."

Nathan knew exactly what his brother wouldn't say out loud over the cell phone. Maybe Mitch was involved in some of the recent manmade fires, if not all of them.

"I would very much like you to get him by the short hairs if you can."

"Yeah," Garrett agreed. "And then shake him. I'll work on it."

Nathan hung up as Joy slipped into the room and set an emergency cup of green tea on his desk. She left again without saying a word. He tried to call Callie, to touch base on this Mitch Michaels development. Her voice mail kicked in.

She's all right, he told himself. Garrett had talked to her a few hours ago. *She just needs some time alone.*

Either that, or she'd already panicked and bolted because they'd made love.

No. She'd said she would be up front with him. He believed her. When she left this time, he'd know about it in advance. That would certainly dull the pain.

He thought about calling the house phone, then decided he needed to get his work done. He'd go over after and see her in person. He had a feeling that was the only way he was going to know what was going on in her head.

THE LANDLINE RANG and Callie jumped. *Nate?* She grabbed for it. "Hello?"

"Callie, I know you're leaving, but can you give me one more day at the school?" Mrs. Serrano. Sounding absolutely desperate. "I already have Principal Domingo covering a class and I don't know what I'm going to do with Mr. Lightfoot's."

"I can't. I'm sorry, but…I can't."

"If it's because of Mr. Gerard…"

Callie rolled her eyes to the ceiling. She'd barely thought of him over the past few days. "No, it's the fire behind my house. I need to be available to investigators."

"The, uh, person in question is no longer in school."

Damn. Word traveled fast in this town. But Garrett had been questioning people in the neighborhood about the car.

"I can't. I'm sorry." Callie hung up after a quick goodbye. She felt for Mrs. Serrano, but she was going to spend the time she had left in town with Nate.

NATE LOOKED UP, surprised to see Callie leaning against the door frame, studying him. He'd been so involved in the story he was working on he hadn't heard her come in.

"Hey," he said in a low voice, feeling ridiculously better because she was there. Safe and...*there.*

She held up a white bag. "You want to partake in some clucks and fries?"

Nathan had a thing for chicken strips—clucks, as they'd called them when they were in high school.

He glanced over at the clock, then saved his story. He was caught up for the day, which was nothing short of a miracle, considering how much he'd had lined up when he'd gotten there, and how shot his concentration was because of Callie and Mitch Michaels. He'd simply put his head down, shut off all thought and forced himself to focus. It had paid off, because now he got to leave with Callie.

"Want to go eat them at my place?"

"You know—" she gave a crooked smile "—I do."

He turned off the monitor, pushed his chair in.

Again Callie followed him to his place in the Neon. She went with him through the side door into the house, and as soon as she had deposited the bag on the table, she was in his arms, her mouth on his. Nathan's leg nearly buckled.

His hands closed over her waist as he regained his balance. Within seconds Callie was unbuttoning his shirt, mumbling something about "always oxford." She peeled it off his shoulders and pushed it down his arms to the cuffs, which she'd forgotten to unbutton. Nathan arched his eyebrows and managed to unbutton himself through the fabric.

"Masterful," Callie said as his shirt hit the floor, followed by her own shirt. And bra. The last time they'd made love it had been dark. Nathan had been hiding his leg. He might still hide his leg, but he was doing better about his less-damaged torso, and right now his attention was on Callie…or rather, her breasts. He boosted her up onto the counter to where he could do them justice. Callie laughed as he lifted her, then sighed as his tongue circled first one nipple and then the other. Her hand clutched his hair.

"Too many clothes," Nathan muttered, unzipping her pants.

"It seems you're more interested in me than in dinner," Callie murmured with a smile.

He considered her, his expression very serious. "Yes, I am."

She laughed again. "Can we go to your bedroom? I like cushioning better than counters."

"We can go anywhere you like." Nathan kissed her. "I'd carry you, but…"

"No need." She jumped down off the counter and walked to the door leading to the hall, her unzipped jeans sliding lower on her hips with each step until her thong showed.

They didn't quite make it to the bedroom. They made it to the carpet, and it was a nice carpet. Plush. Perfect. But neither of them was thinking about carpeting when Nathan pulled off her thong and nudged her legs apart. Callie clung to him as he thrust into her, wishing they'd made peace weeks ago. So much wasted time.

It wasn't until later, when they lay side by side on the floor catching their breath, that Callie ran a hand over the rug and asked, "Did you pay extra for double padding?"

"Yeah, I did."

"Good planning."

He stood and held out a hand to help Callie to her feet. "Shower, then chicken?"

"Will the shower involve creative use of suds?"

He grinned. "Doesn't it always?"

Afterward they ate the chicken and fries without bothering to warm them, and talked about the old times, the good times, everything except the present.

It was Nathan who finally brought it up, after they'd abandoned the kitchen and made love yet again, in his bed. Garrett had contacted Callie that afternoon, so she knew about Mitch and the alibi. She did not know how concerned Nathan was.

"If it hadn't been an alibi, he'd be out on bail," Callie pointed out.

"True." Nate propped his head on his elbow. "Maybe you should stay here."

"I, uh…"

"Is that scarier than facing Mitch?" he asked, watching her expression shift from wary to warier.

"No. Of course not. It's just that I've never really depended on anyone for anything, except for Grace."

He reached out and pulled her to him. It took her a moment to settle at his side, her head on his chest, but her muscles weren't fully relaxed. "What do you do when you fall in love?"

"I try not to do that," she said softly, her breath teasing his skin.

"Why?" he asked. Why couldn't she let herself fall in love with him?

"It's the way I am."

He was getting tired of hearing that answer. Nathan didn't buy absolutes.

"Do you think it has something to do with being a foster kid? With security?" he ventured, tossing out the obvious theory, the one he'd always believed was at the bottom of Callie's wanderlust.

She settled her head again. "Grace gave me all the

security I needed. If she hadn't, then I wouldn't exactly be the type to gallivant around the world, would I? Especially with my father being an unsolved missing person case."

They'd discussed her father and the possibilities innumerable times as teens. She'd always seemed so matter-of-fact about the situation, so accepting of what she couldn't change, even if that meant accepting that her father had probably been murdered. Even now her tone was dispassionate.

"And you don't think what happened to him might affect your sense of security?"

"Whatever happened to him had nothing to do with me. He was in the wrong place at the wrong time, or maybe even involved in the wrong profession. The only thing that possibly relates is he needed to travel. Just like me, so I guess I inherited that trait from him."

Funny that the trait never showed up until graduation, after Nathan had told her he loved her.

"No offense, Callie, but I'm not buying it."

Her fingers curled on his chest and he felt her inhale deeply, then exhale. "Don't psychoanalyze me, Nate. Does it really matter why?"

"If you know the reason, then you can change."

She brought her head up suddenly. "Who says I want to change?"

"Is it healthy to run every time someone gets too close?"

"I don't run because people get too close."

"Then why? And I don't want to hear it's the way you are. There's a reason and I don't for one minute believe it's in your DNA."

Callie's expression was a mixture of anger and pain. "Why are you ruining things? Why can't we just enjoy what we have?"

Because we could have so much more.

Nathan bit back the words. For now. After he'd remained silent for a few moments, Callie finally relaxed and curled up against him again, her cheek and her lightly clenched fist resting on his chest. She stared pensively off across the room until finally her eyes drifted shut and she slept.

CHAPTER FOURTEEN

NATHAN AND HIS BROTHERS took their father out for an early breakfast before work. At first John acted as if the breakfast was a setup, but eventually he let down his guard—right up to the point when Garrett reordered for him, nixing the country fried steak, fries and gravy for an egg white omelet and fruit.

"He's supposed to be the killjoy," John grumbled, stabbing a finger at Nathan. Nate shrugged it off. As always. He'd developed a fairly thick skin over the years, which had proved handy in a journalism career.

"I want to be the killjoy next time," Seth declared. John growled at him and picked up his glass of ice water.

They discussed the fire at Callie's place, which John had not been involved with, until the food came, then launched into the parts of the investigation Garrett could discuss. In other words, the parts that Nathan was free to print. Garrett mentioned that he'd arranged for additional patrols in that neighborhood, then shot a look at Nate before adding that he wasn't entirely certain they were needed.

"She slept at her place last night," Nathan said, not mentioning that he'd been there, too. They hadn't discussed the past or the future. They'd simply given each other as much pleasure as possible. In fact, they'd barely spoken. Things had changed since he'd told her he didn't buy the genetic wanderlust theory, and Nathan had no idea what the outcome would be. He was certain, however, that he and Callie would never have any chance of a future until she faced whatever it was that made her run.

John jerked his gaze up from the fruit he'd been pushing around the bowl. Nathan waited for him to say something—anything—disparaging, because this time it was not going unchallenged. His dad pulled in a deep, disapproving breath, but said nothing.

All in all, it was a crappy father-sons meal, and Nathan was glad to escape to his stressful job. He'd been there almost five minutes when Joy brought in a cup of tea—the caffeinated kind—and two aspirin. Nathan hadn't asked for aspirin, so his sleepless night coupled with breakfast with his dad might have showed. He thanked her and she left, after giving him one final worried look. A few seconds later she buzzed him.

"Mr. Michaels on line one."

Nathan wished he had that flask of Laphroaig. He pushed his hair back off his forehead, then picked up the office line.

"Marcenek."

"Nathan, I wanted to touch base concerning these unfounded accusations against Mitch."

"There were witnesses." And Nate had already written the story.

"One of whom was eight years old. And we both know the veracity of eyewitnesses. What they saw was someone who looked similar—if they saw anyone at all. Mitch was home with the family."

Funny how rich people's sight was more dependable than other people's. And Nathan wasn't going to bring up the distinctive sports car Mitch drove, which several people had spotted in the area. There were only two in town and Garrett had checked the other one out, too.

"Your boy needs help, Vince."

"One more remark like that and you're no longer an employee of our news family." Which was very likely going to happen whether Nate made another remark or not. He was so ready to move on.

"You want me to pretend this didn't happen."

"There is no concrete proof it did happen."

The guy sounded as if he was practicing a speech.

"I have to report the news. If the sheriff questions a person of interest in a felony, it's news. It's up to the sheriff whether or not he releases the name."

Vince's voice became flintlike. "Keep Mitch out of this. He wasn't involved. Not a word." Vince ended the call without saying goodbye.

Nathan set the phone on his desk and brought up his

computer screen. He started to type but his fingers stilled on the keyboard after a couple of sentences.

So what did he want to be when he grew up? He should probably make a decision on that, because he would eventually be printing Mitch's name, if Garrett was correct in his assumptions, and then he'd no longer be the editor of the *Wesley Star*.

He reached for his cell and found Suzanne's work number.

"I need a job," he said without a hello.

"It's about time. Too bad you didn't need a job last month."

"Things have changed. Got any leads?"

"I might. The guy they just hired isn't going to last."

"Why not?"

"Because the editor is going to kill him. He writes like a dream, but he's all ego. Real prima donna and it isn't going over well. The guy is oblivious."

The wonder of the superego. "Is it wrong of me to hope for the worst?"

"Naw," Suzanne said. "The guy is digging his own grave fast. I'll call when there's a development, and in the meanwhile…maybe you could get away for a day, come and meet some people?"

"Yeah. I can do that." And, while he waited for a job opening, he had some resources to support himself. He'd received an injury settlement for his leg, which he'd invested. His house payment was low enough that he could rent the place for the cost of the payment and then some. If he wanted to head off to the city to try his hand at freelancing—either editing or writing—until something permanent opened up, well, he could do it.

So…what did he do about Callie?

NATHAN WAS A QUIET GUY, but tonight he was too quiet for Callie's peace of mind. They were in his bed, where they seemed to spend most of their time together, laughing, talking, making love. Only tonight they weren't laughing or talking.

Something was on his mind. Something more than what they'd just finished doing, which was uppermost in her mind at the moment.

"What's up?" she finally asked, tracing a pattern in his chest hair until he caught her fingers and brought them to kiss his lips.

"I'm trying to get a job in Seattle."

Callie's head came up. "When?"

He continued to hold her hand loosely in his own. "As soon as I can."

She settled her cheek back onto his chest. They'd discussed Vince threatening to fire him and she really hoped Nathan sued for wrongful dismissal if that happened. He had an article coming out in this week's paper, but the sheriff's office hadn't officially named a suspect. They figured Nate would be employed right up until a suspect was named and Nate reported it.

"What do you think about Seattle?" he asked.

She frowned. "What do you mean?"

"I was thinking that maybe you wouldn't mind going there."

"I…uh…"

"It wouldn't have to be a big commitment, Callie."

She moistened her suddenly dry lips. He wanted her to go with him. It would be like it was now. Only in Seattle.

Why was that so scary?

Because he was talking as if they would live together and maybe depend on each other and…

"I don't think that would be good."

"Why?" he asked in a no-nonsense voice.

"Because if I wanted to leave and we had gone there together…"

"Then I imagine you would just do it." He rolled over and took her face in his hands. "Do you care about me, Callie?"

"You know I do," she whispered back. "You're my best friend."

"But you don't trust me."

Or was it that she didn't trust herself?

Callie pulled away from Nate and got out of bed. She needed to move, to do something. "I have to go."

Nate didn't try to stop her. She put on her clothes while he lay in bed watching her, his expression blank, as if this was exactly what he had expected.

"You can't run forever. We need to talk about this."

"Talk about what?"

"What makes you run."

"I know what makes me run, whether you believe it or not."

Nate got out of bed and started getting dressed himself.

"Sometimes I wonder which of us is more scarred," he muttered as he stepped into his jeans.

"I am not scarred. You just can't accept who I am."

"But I do love you."

Callie froze for a split second, then forced herself to shove her feet into her shoes, her arms into her jacket sleeves. She couldn't remember the last time she'd heard words that frightened her more.

"YOU ARE THE LUCKIEST SOB I know," Suzanne said.

Funny, but he wasn't feeling all that lucky since having his Seattle conversation with Callie the night before. But the paper had come out with the article about the unnamed arson suspect, and Vince hadn't fired him for that, so maybe he did have a little luck going his way.

"Did they get rid of the ego guy?" Nathan asked, shuffling through some hard copies on his desk.

"No. Jessica McCrae quit. She got accepted into law school and she's outta here."

Nate let out a low whistle.

"She gave notice today and they want to fill the position immediately." Suzanne paused before saying, "I, uh, took the liberty of tossing your name into the ring.

Reynolds would like to see a résumé and a warm body if you can swing a quick trip up here."

"Marcus Reynolds?"

"The same."

Marcus had been Nate's immediate boss before he was injured, and they had always seen eye to eye. "Give me a date and time and I'll work something out."

"Fax a résumé and I'll get back to you."

Nathan hung up the phone. He was fond of Wesley, understood the people, and he liked living close to his brothers. But he wasn't an editor at heart. He was a writer and reporter.

Which left the question…did he quit? Or wait to get fired? Because he had no doubt he was going to be fired in the near future. Vince trusted him to do exactly as he was told—that point was driven home when his boss hadn't demanded to see the last edition of the paper before it came out—so Vince was going to be furious when Nathan eventually defied his orders and printed Mitch's name as a suspect. On the plus side, if he got fired he'd get severance, but just how much of an effect would that have on his chances in Seattle?

Reynolds would understand.

The phone rang just as Nate turned back to the keyboard.

"Day after tomorrow," Suzanne said. "Can you do it?"

Chip could take over his job for two days. Three if

he had to, and Nathan probably wouldn't be working for Vince Michaels by that time.

"I can do it."

NATHAN HADN'T SEEN CALLIE in two days—not since he'd told her he loved her—when he stopped by her house. There was a For Sale sign on the lawn, but the Neon was still out front. He knocked on the door.

Callie answered almost immediately. When she saw it was him, her lips compressed, but she stepped back to let him in.

He looked down at her, wishing there was some magic way to get beyond this barrier Callie didn't believe in.

"I'm going to Seattle."

Callie's mouth dropped open. "Travel safe," she finally said.

"Will you be here when I get back?"

"I don't know. I had an offer for a travel story that might last two weeks. Argentina."

"Is that what you want, Callie?"

"It's what I *do*. I travel." She tilted her chin defensively.

"You're just like your father," he said softly.

"I know."

"He abandoned everyone, and you do the same thing."

Callie's head jerked as if he'd slapped her. "My father didn't abandon me!" she snapped. "He always came back, until the trip when he *couldn't* come back."

"You know that how…?"

"I…" Callie closed her mouth.

"Even if he *was* a crime victim, the fact remains your father dumped you with whoever was available, while he went off to wherever he used to go. That's abandonment. You aren't hardwired to travel, Callie. You're hardwired to protect yourself. You live this way because it helps you believe your father was an okay guy. It helps you feel close to him."

"My father *was* an okay guy."

"Okay guys don't dump their kids with whoever's available and take off. Why do you think you were so upset about the Hobart kids?"

She turned her head sideways, looking away.

"All I'm saying is that maybe you're trying to justify your father's actions by living them. And maybe you don't have to do that anymore."

Callie pushed her hand up over her forehead as if she had a headache.

"Callie—" He reached to touch her face, but she stepped away.

"Go on your trip, Nate."

Nathan let his hand drop back to his side. "Will you be here when I get back?"

"I don't know, and that's as up front as I can truthfully be right now."

Ten minutes later, Nathan made the turn onto the highway to Elko, his mind absorbed with Callie—as it would be all night. And the next day. Smooth. Really smooth.

He wondered if he'd ever see her again.

CALLIE CLEARED EVERYTHING out of the house in preparation for the sale. She boxed up the dishes she'd been using, the teapot and extra towels, and took them over to Alice, who was planning a yard sale and was quite thrilled to have additional items.

"Are you sure you don't want me to give you the money they bring in?" she asked for the second time. The kitchen was now empty except for paper plates and plastic forks.

"No. This is a thank-you for being such a good friend to Grace," Callie said. Then she went back to rake the backyard, which she'd finally gotten mowed. The man across the alley, who'd also rebuilt the fence for a reasonable sum in less than half a day, had taken care of the job.

She threw herself into the work. It gave her body something to do while her mind ran wild. Try as she might, she could not shut out the things Nate had said to her.

She wanted him to be wrong. She didn't want her father to be a guy who abandoned her. She wanted him to be the same kind of gypsy she was.

And Nathan had no reason to question the theory that her dad had been the victim of foul play. Grace had believed it, and Grace was one of the most intelligent women Callie had ever met. She was a woman who liked to learn things. She read broadly and when she didn't know about something, she researched.

She must have done the same in the situation with Callie's father. Callie couldn't imagine Grace doing less. She also couldn't imagine her not prodding the police to find answers.

Yet Callie didn't recall any information in Grace's extensive files, the ones that had taken her most of a day to sort, on unsolved police cases. And Grace had told her she hadn't known where her father was headed on that fateful trip.

Did that make sense? Would Grace take Callie without knowing where her dad was going? What if there had been an emergency? What if Grace had had to get hold of him?

That didn't add up.

Damn Nate for bringing this up. Callie had dealt with the loss of her father long ago. She didn't need to be obsessing about it now.

But she had a feeling that it was, indeed, at the bottom of everything.

CHAPTER FIFTEEN

NATE WOULD HAVE ENJOYED his stay in the city more if he'd been able to get Callie off his mind.

Would she be there when he got back? Or was he going to have to hunt her down? Because he would this time.

"What's going on?" Suzanne finally asked over drinks on his last evening there. It was after ten on a weeknight, but the hotel bar was still busy. The meeting with Marcus had gone well, and Nate was fairly certain he'd be called back for an interview. He wanted the job. He also wanted to keep Callie.

"Unfinished business," he said.

"I'm sure the paper will get along just fine without you."

Nate nodded, swirled the ice in his almost empty drink.

"Another?" Suzanne nodded at the glass.

He surveyed the assortment of liquor displayed on backlit glass shelves behind the sleek curve of the ebony bar—a far cry from the haphazardly arranged bottles on the homemade wooden shelves in Fuzzy's Tavern—then shook his head.

"I think I'm good." Nathan preferred to do his thinking while sober, and right now he had some things to work out.

"You're a lot of fun on vacation."

He smiled then and she smiled back. They did well together, he and Suzanne. "I'd like to work for Marcus," he said. "I'd like to move back to Seattle."

"But…"

"No buts. I would."

"But…"

"I think I'm in love."

"When will you know for sure?" Suzanne asked drily.

"The thing is," Nathan said, ignoring her last comment, "she has a problem."

Suzanne pantomimed lifting a bottle to her lips, and Nathan frowned. "Wouldn't you feel stupid if that was the problem?"

"Is it?" she asked, her eyes growing wide.

"No. She's afraid of commitment. Her father disappeared when she was young and I think that's why she's always on the move."

"I don't get the connection," Suzanne said. "If her father left, don't you think that would make her more clingy?"

"I think she's validating his abandonment somehow in her head."

"What are you going to do?"

"No idea. I don't even know if she'll be there when I get back."

"Don't waste your time on a flake."

"She's not a flake."

Suzanne tilted her head. "Maybe you are in love. I've never seen you in love before."

Nathan made a face at her, then finished the last of his drink. Suzanne glanced at her watch.

"Better get home to Julia," he said, wishing he could go home to Callie right now instead of waiting for his flight the next day.

"You could have stopped by the condo, you know. She doesn't blame you anymore."

But she had at the time of the accident and Nate knew how ingrained a certain behavior could become. Being the good brother because it was the only role your father halfway understood. Or letting memories of a long-dead father control the way you lived.

"Maybe next time."

"I'll hold you to that."

Nathan grinned. "You do that."

THE DREAM CAME BACK full force that night, scaring the bejeezus out of Callie. It was the closest she'd come to remembering—and for one terrifying moment she thought she had. There was a flash of strong recognition, an overwhelming sense of "of course!" followed by the withdrawal, the terror.

Callie jumped out of bed, pacing the floor, hugging herself.

Oh, man. Oh, man.

This had to stop. She had to get out of Wesley and away from Nate.

But this time Nate hadn't triggered the dream. She was certain of it. And the Hobarts probably weren't guilty, either. The kids were cared for in the family's own way.

That left…questions. Lots of questions about the dream and, quite possibly, her father.

So who did she ask?

Who would know about her dad? No one in this town. They'd lived in Elko, sixty miles away, and before that Reno, and before that…who knew? Somewhere along the line her mother had died. Callie had been four at the time. The story was she'd drowned, but right now Callie didn't believe anything anymore.

Okay, when she came to live with Grace, CPS would have been involved, but it would have been the Elko CPS. Would they still have files that old? And law enforcement would have been called when her dad hadn't returned from his trip.

Twenty-two years ago, so most if not all of the deputies would be retired. Maybe she could find the case file in Elko?

Or maybe she could ask the only person she knew who'd been involved in law enforcement at the time.

And wouldn't John Marcenek be thrilled to have a visit from her?

John was not thrilled. He didn't even try to fake it. He opened the door and, when Callie told him she had a few questions, he gruffly waved her into the house, as if she were interrupting high tea with the queen.

"Why are you here?" he asked, easing his bulk down onto a sturdy captain's chair.

"I want information about my father."

"I didn't know your father. He wasn't from around here."

"Do you know of him?"

John shook his head stubbornly.

"Grace never had you look into his disappearance?"

"She did."

"And...?" Callie prompted, growing impatient.

"Nothing came of it."

Callie's jaw tightened, but she'd questioned too many difficult people over the course of her career to let John Marcenek buffalo her.

"But you helped Grace with some kind of foster care issue. I once heard her tell a friend about it."

"All I did was help the Elko authorities track Grace down," he said dismissively.

Callie stared at him. "Why would they have tracked Grace down?" She felt a numb premonitory chill spreading through her. His statement made no sense. "My father left me at her house."

"Your father left you in the Elko K-Mart."

Callie blinked, not comprehending. Surely she'd heard wrong. After all, blood was pounding in her ears to the point that she was starting to feel light-headed. She swallowed hard. "No. He left me with Grace."

"The night crew found you asleep under a clothing rack after the store had closed." He glared at her impatiently. "You were six years old, for cripe's sake. Don't tell me you don't remember?"

Callie wanted very much to tell him she didn't remember, but her voice didn't seem to be working. Neither did her brain. She stared at him for a long, long moment before she managed to get control of her vocal cords. "Does Nate know?"

John Marcenek gave her a disgusted, of-course-he-does look.

Callie jumped to her feet then, knocking the chair back and walked blindly to the door.

"Wait a minute!"

Callie ignored him and headed out the door, down the path to her car. She didn't know at what point she'd started running, or even how she got the car started. John was lumbering toward her when she squealed away from the curb.

Stay or go? The question circled in Callie's brain as she started to drive. Her suitcase was already in the car. Heck, everything she owned was in the car.

Stay or go?

THERE WAS SOMETHING WRONG with the old man. When Nathan got home he went over to his dad's house to see him before going to the office, since both Garrett and Seth were on shift. John was sitting in his chair at the table, a solitaire game laid out in front of him. But he had yet to turn a card.

"Are you feeling all right?" Nathan asked.

"How was the trip?"

"Interesting."

"Are you going to leave?" he asked bluntly.

"When the right job comes along."

"No idea when that might be? Or where?"

Nate shook his head. "Could be a while. Could be tomorrow."

John stared off into space.

"Come on, Dad. It isn't as if I'm thirteen and running off to join the circus."

"I like having all of you here."

Well, that was a shocker. Nate tilted his head as he gave his dad a sidelong glance. Yep. It did appear to be his father sitting there, staring at the table.

"Garrett, Seth and you," the old man continued, as if there might be some confusion as to who he was referring to. "I like having you around."

"Yeah," Nathan said. Had the old man had another episode?

"Callie was here."

"She was?" Nathan asked cautiously, not liking his father's odd tone.

"Yeah. I, uh, told her something I don't think she knew."

"How bad of a something?"

John glanced down at the cards. He reached out and put a red ten on a black jack, then settled his hand back in his lap before looking up at his son. Nathan stared at him. What on earth? His heart wasn't beating faster, but it was beating harder. It felt as if it was hitting his rib cage with each slow pulse.

"What did you tell her, Dad?"

"I told her that her father abandoned her in the Elko K-Mart."

For one long moment, Nathan simply stared at his father, not quite able to believe what he'd heard. John stared back in defiance.

"I thought she knew, damn it. I thought she was putting on some stupid act to get information out of me."

"Her father left her in a store?" *This was crazy.*

"They found her sleeping under a clothes rack after hours. She was six years old." His father dropped his chin, slowly shook his head. "Hell, I remember stuff from when I was six years old and that was almost sixty years ago."

Nathan shoved his hands in his pockets and turned to stare blindly out the window. Her father had abandoned her in a store? Some things were falling into place. He muttered a curse.

"You remember stuff when you were six, right?" John asked.

"Yeah." He remembered Callie when she came into Mrs. Milliken's first grade class, with her long blond braids, and baggy tights over her skinny legs.

"Then what the hell?"

"Dad. You're a cop. You know about traumatic memory loss."

"That happens in car wrecks, beatings. Not from falling asleep in a store."

"Who knows how terrifying it might have been to wake up in a store? To be surrounded by strangers. Especially for a kid who didn't have the most stable existence." He took a few paces to the door, then pulled his cell out of his pocket and hit her number. No answer. But he hadn't expected one. "How did she look when she left?"

"Upset," John confessed.

Nathan cursed and paced some more. "What the hell were you thinking?"

"I told you what I was thinking. I was thinking she knew and was pumping me for information."

"What kind of information?"

"I don't know!" his father bellowed. John Marcenek was not accustomed to being wrong, and this time he'd screwed up and he knew it.

"Why didn't you tell me?"

"Why? Grace asked me to keep the facts quiet. She and I were the only ones who knew."

"Why the secrecy?"

John gave him a withering look. "Grace thought it would be easier on Callie."

"Well, she was probably right," Nathan admitted. People would have been all over a story like that. Instead of being involved with a mystery, Callie would have been the object of pity, and heaven only knew what kids would do with ammo like that if they hadn't liked her. Kids were ruthless creatures.

"You could have told me after she left town that first time. It wouldn't have mattered then."

"Why should I have told you?"

Nathan turned an incredulous gaze toward his dad. "Because it might have helped me understand why she left."

"So you could have gone after her? Tried to fix things?" John demanded.

"Yeah. Maybe," Nathan answered in the same tone. "It was my choice. I was eighteen."

"Oh, yeah. Eighteen-year-olds are known for brains." John shoved the cards into a messy heap in front of him. "That girl had issues. There was no way I wanted you chasing after her."

"I loved her."

"You were better off without her," his dad said bitterly.

"How so?"

"The writing and all that shit. You never wanted to do that until you hooked up with her. You were planning to go into forensics. It was the one thing you were interested in that I understood. And then along came Callie and all that was out the window."

"I always liked to write. Like Mom did. I just never said it out loud. Callie had nothing to do with it."

John snorted.

Nathan didn't give a flying you-know-what what his dad believed. He started for the door.

"Where you going?" his father asked, even though he had to know the answer.

"I'm going to find Callie. It's what I should have done the last time." Although neither of them would have been prepared to fight this battle back then. Now…now there was a chance.

He hoped.

NATHAN DROVE to Callie's house. As he expected, the Neon was gone. He walked past the For Sale sign and went to the door to knock. Just to be sure. The Hobart kids were playing in their yard. He could hear them arguing over a ball, which soon came sailing over the thick honeysuckle bushes and rolled to a stop in the vacant lot. Nathan walked over to it just as the kids came out of the yard. They stopped when they saw him.

"Have you seen the lady who lives here?"

The children looked at each other, then simultaneously shrugged. They had been taught not to talk to strangers. They were also skinny and dusty, and he could understand how Callie, having seen them out after dark, when Grandma had fallen asleep, would have been concerned. Especially since she had a deeply ingrained reason to be sensitive to neglect.

"If you've seen her today, nod your heads."

The girl nodded and the boy shook his head.

"Great. Thanks." Nathan went back to his car and hit Garrett's number on speed dial. "I want to know the name and address of the owner of Callie's Neon. And don't tell me you have no way of knowing, because you ran the plate. If you didn't, then you're some kind of pod person impersonating my brother, the anal cop."

"I'll drop the information by after shift."

"I want it now."

"I'm on patrol. I'll be at your place in ninety minutes. If you can wait that long."

Nathan didn't want to wait that long. He'd waited over a decade to straighten things out with Callie.

THE NEON WAS PARKED in the driveway. His driveway. Nathan was barely aware of getting out of his truck and crossing to the kitchen door through the open garage. Callie was sitting at the table, her laptop in front of her, the lid down. For a moment they just stared at one another. Then Callie spoke.

"Your father is such a jerk."

Nathan stopped, his hand on the back of the chair

across the table from Callie's. "I'm sorry he did what he did, Callie."

"He tried to make me think you knew about my dad and didn't tell me. He doesn't understand you at all."

Nathan tilted his head to one side. This was not what he expected. "But I think he likes me," he said slowly, studying her. *Finally.*

"Then I guess you're better off than me," she said.

She stared down at the table. Nathan waited, but when she didn't look up, he finally asked, "Why are you here? At my place?"

She seemed shell-shocked as she raised her eyes and said, "I think I'm in the process of staying."

"Callie." He opened his arms. She rose from the chair and walked around the table and straight into his embrace.

"Oh, man, Nate." She leaned into him and he tightened his embrace. "You had it nailed. I was doing what my dad did. I was abandoning before I got abandoned."

"I kind of figured that."

"I have this dream. I've had it forever, but I could never remember it. It would come when I was stressed or anxious, scare the heck out of me. I've been having it so often while I was here. I thought it was because of you."

"Same dream every time?"

"I shouldn't call it a dream, because it's more like a flashback. A moment of recognition and terror. I had it before I went to stay with Grace, so I was certain it wasn't related to what happened to my dad…"

She rubbed her forehead. "I figured it out. I know what it is now. It's a flash of waking up under all the shirts on the clothes rack when my dad left me in that store, and seeing hands coming at me. I had no idea what was happening, where I was. I didn't know where my dad was. I was supposed to wait for him and they were taking me somewhere…." She stilled, staring sightlessly across the room. Finally she pulled in a deep breath and exhaled. "The first dream wasn't a dream at all. It was real. And the other dreams were flashbacks I wouldn't let myself remember." She sighed against his shirt. "I guess I'm glad I went to talk to your dad, even if it was traumatic."

"He could have gone at it a little more tactfully." Nate hesitated. "I figured after he did that, you'd be long gone by now."

"I started to leave," Callie confessed. "I drove almost twenty miles. It felt wrong. I mean—" she lifted her head so she could look into his eyes "—really wrong. This was a problem I couldn't outrun. This is a problem I'm going to have to face." She bit her lip. "I'm going to break the McCarran cycle."

"I'll help."

She leaned her cheek against his chest and he stroked her hair. "I'm so sorry, Nate."

"Don't be."

"You trusted me with your leg and even then I trusted you with…nothing."

"You had reasons."

"Which were a bunch of made-up crap." She tilted her head back to look into his face.

"Self-protective made-up crap."

She choked out a small laugh. "Yeah. I had this brilliant strategy. I'd make up excuses for my knee-jerk reactions instead of trying to find out why I acted that way."

"Did you have any clue about what your dad had done?"

"Just the dream."

Nate pushed the hair away from her face. "Well, I happen to know a little about self-protection myself. And I know that while it's hard to overcome those impulses, you can. Maybe not with everyone right away, but with certain—" he gently kissed her lips "—special—" he kissed her again "—people. The people you love and trust."

She smiled against his mouth. "What exactly are you saying, Nate?"

"That if you hang around with me, we can whip this together."

She drew back slightly. "And what about your father and your brother? You know…the ones who like me so much?"

Nate touched his forehead to hers, loving that she showed no sign of backing away, putting up the barriers. "You'll get used to them. I did."

"Garrett told me you took the job where you got hurt to prove to me you weren't boring."

Nathan made a mental note to kill his brother. "It may have entered into the equation," he admitted. "I wouldn't have minded becoming a dynamic guy who you regretted dumping."

"I never stopped regretting leaving you. Trust me. But I thought it was the only way things could be, that one of us would have devastated the other if I'd stayed."

"I'm not going to leave you, Callie, and I hope you never leave me. We can go places, we can stay here. I don't care."

"Let's go to where you have a job." She pushed her hands into his hair as she tilted her lips up to lightly touch his. "Because I can always—"

"Find temp work."

"Except with you," she said just before she kissed him. "I plan on this being a permanent job."

Nathan gathered her closer, pressing her body against his, not caring one bit about scars. "With full benefits," he murmured.

"Exactly."

* * * * *

Harlequin Intrigue top author
Delores Fossen presents
a brand-new series of breathtaking romantic suspense!
TEXAS MATERNITY: HOSTAGES
The first installment available May 2010:
THE BABY'S GUARDIAN

Shaw cursed and hooked his arm around Sabrina.

Despite the urgency that the deadly gunfire created, he tried to be careful with her, and he took the brunt of the fall when he pulled her to the ground. His shoulder hit hard, but he held on tight to his gun so that it wouldn't be jarred from his hand.

Shaw didn't stop there. He crawled over Sabrina, sheltering her pregnant belly with his body, and he came up ready to return fire.

This was obviously a situation he'd wanted to avoid at all cost. He didn't want his baby in the middle of a fight with these armed fugitives, but when they fired that shot, they'd left him no choice. Now, the trick was to get Sabrina safely out of there.

"Get down," someone on the SWAT team yelled from the roof of the adjacent building.

Shaw did. He dropped lower, covering Sabrina as best he could.

There was another shot, but this one came from a

rifleman on the SWAT team. Shaw didn't look up, but he heard the sound of glass being blown apart.

The shots continued, all coming from his men, which meant it might be time to try to get Sabrina to better cover. Shaw glanced at the front of the building.

So that Sabrina's pregnant belly wouldn't be smashed against the ground, Shaw eased off her and moved her to a sitting position so that her back was against the brick wall. They were close. Too close. And face-to-face.

He found himself staring right into those sea-green eyes.

How will Shaw get Sabrina out?
Follow the daring rescue and the heartbreaking
aftermath in THE BABY'S GUARDIAN
by Delores Fossen,
available May 2010 from Harlequin Intrigue.